PROBE8

8 MODERN MYSTERIES OF DETECTIVE FICTION

NIDHI ARORA

Made with ♥ on the Notion Press Platform
www.notionpress.com

To

Ishaan and Deshant

Contents

Foreword

By Rashmi Bansal

To write detective fiction, one needs a devious mind. That was my thinking, at least, before I met Nidhi Arora.

Intelligent, soft-spoken, responsible, and sensitive - was my impression when she did the workshop and wrote her first story set in a village in Uttarakhand. Wo bhi shudh Hindi mein. (That too, in pure Hindi).

But over the next few months, as she churned out stories for the Writers Gym program: layer by layer, a different Nidhi was revealed. A murder, then a second. Hey Bhagwan, aise ideas isey aatey kahan se hain!

Well, that's the power of imagination. Slowly extending into the emerging world of AI, Nidhi's writing took on a sci-fi flavour. One of my all-time favourite genres!

One of the unique things about Nidhi is that her brain lights up when she receives a writing prompt. She doesn't procrastinate till the last day, last minute. Usi waqt, usi din submission aa jaata hai.

As her mentor and cheerleader, I am delighted to see the steady progress Nidhi has made in a short span of time. At times, she gets a little carried away and writes extra-long stories. And when there is a tendency to show off all the research she's put in to get the technical bits right. But whenever I've pointed this out, she's been quick to incorporate the feedback and improve her story. That, ultimately, is the hallmark of a writer who wants each story to be better than her last one.

I am sure you will enjoy reading her first collection of short stories. And many more to come. Let that beautiful mind keep whirring and stirring and producing delicious, salacious, audacious stories.

Enjoy!

Rashmi Bansal
February 2023

Preface

While talking to clients in my consulting journey, the most striking thing was the gap in knowledge about how data was being used. It was like I lived in two worlds at the same time – one that was working every minute to protect the world from the ever-evolving cyber-crime, and the other that lived blissfully unaware until it hit them – Smack! And then it was too late.

These stories just happened on their own. I thought this would be a fun way to introduce friends to the actual potential of new technology and its use – both in solving and facilitating crimes.

The readers liked them, and here they are.

Enjoy!

Nidhi

February 2023

PS: Nothing in this book is in the realm of fantasy, especially in the stories on AI. Every behaviour of or using AI that you read in the book – has either already happened, or can happen using the current technology.

Acknowledgements

First, of course, to my writing mentor, **Rashmi Bansal**, who is the reason this book was even conceived. It is to her that one owes the genesis of the short story writer in me.

Everyone in the **Writer's Gym** who read the stories and shared feedback.

The next is **Ishaan**, the child who patiently read all my stories and gave the go ahead – that they do belong in a book. If this book is out here, it is thanks to this young man who was convinced that these stories deserve to be read. And he is a wise young man.

Swati Lodha, who freely shared her wisdom as a bestselling author. **Upasana Arora**, who has been an inspiration from the day I met her.

T Sat, who patiently hand-held me through the journey, answering noob questions with patience.

Avijit, for his suggestion on the title. **Manisha,** for encouraging me to publish these, and for her positive feedback on the stories.

Avijit, Manisha, Amita, Rita ji, and Sunil ji, for their unflinching support on everything – from feedback on the name of the book to the cover page. These four friends formed the core group to which I went back for all advice – from random advice to general self-doubt.

Maithreyi, my pillar of support.

My family – Deshant, Ishaan, Mom, Miki, Mani, Gini, Angad, Mom and Dad.... As D says (accurately) – the three priorities of my life are – family, family, family, in that order.

My editor, **Jalpa Shah,** who is a professional one is lucky to work with in a lifetime. She did this entire project in record time. She made this book so much better through her inputs.

To **Dall-e2** and the other AI image generators that have created illustrations for this book.

About This Book

Nidhi's stories are 'smart crime' thrillers ....relatable, cautionary tales.

The crisp and clear writing is full of promise for Indian readers.

Swati Lodha
Bestselling author

Unique plots, interesting situations, innovative formats, gripping contemporary stories on well-researched subjects.

Nidhi Arora's first story collection may be the first milestone in her life but some of the stories reflect a seasoned writer in her. Her writing certainly has the potential to go miles ahead.

Keep writing Nidhi! Look forward to your new collection of stories or a novel soon. Best wishes!

- Viky Arya
Author and Poet

With technology, the nature of crime has changed, and we, the readers, need crime fiction that reflects this reality. Loved reading each story. Fabulous job!

Deshant Kaila
India MD, Pepsico GBS

Nidhi Arora's collection of stories is captivating, thoughtful, and keeps you hooked to the narrative. I'm still dipping my toes in the fiction pool and trying to figure out what works and what doesn't but these pieces caught my attention and I could not help but finish reading all of them one after another. All of her stories were incredibly well written, and I wish her all the best in her future endeavours and may she continue to write such amazing pieces.

Upasana Arora
Director, Yashoda Hospitals

CHAPTER ONE

MR. VENKAT REDDY

"Mr. Venkat Reddy? Any passenger here named Mr. Venkat Reddy?" the airline staff came to boarding gate B1 and called out. No one responded.

Neither at B2. Nor at A2 or A1.

"Mr. Venkat Reddy? Are you here, Mr. Venkat Reddy?" thirty minutes later, the voice boomed again. Same airline, different staff. No one stirred. Anywhere.

****

"Hello?! Is that Mr. Shailesh? From Ashish Associates?" the voice had an urgency that Shailesh could not ignore. "Yes, this is Shailesh from Ashish." He replied.

"Do you know where Venkat is?" the voice asked.

"Errm.. in office, I guess? Who's this please?"

"I am Venkat's wife. Took your number from the office board after great difficulty. Venkat is not in office. He has not called me from Kolkata even. The hotel he was supposed to check into has no information about him. They say it was a no show."

"Sorry, sorry, please come again and try and speak a little slower. What is Venkat doing in Kolkata? And, what is your name?"

"Sorry, my name is Latha. Venkat was supposed to be in Kolkata this week for work, no? Last night, he left for the airport, and since it was a late-night flight, I told him to message me after checking into the hotel. But when I woke up in the morning, there was no message.

That's when I got concerned. His phone is coming switched off. His WhatsApp last seen is at 8:30 PM last night, when he might have reached the airport."

Shailesh was nonplussed, but he thought fast on his feet. "Latha, please listen to me carefully. Do you have your family with you? Is there anyone who can come with you to the office? Please make sure you don't come alone. Do bring a family member with you, preferably a lady."

"Why are you saying like this? Is something not OK with my Venkat?" Latha's voice faltered.

"No Latha. This is standard operating protocol. We cannot interact with female family members without the presence of at least one other lady, preferably from their own family. This is our company's rule." Shailesh was telling a white lie, but in this case, it was necessary.

"Ok, I will be right over. Be there in 15." If anxiety had a voice, this would be it.

****

25 minutes later, Shailesh, his Executive Assistant, Navita, Latha, and her friend, Vandita, were seated in a cosy conference room. Navita had arranged breakfast for everyone.

"Latha, please tell us from the beginning. What did Venkat tell you about the travel?"

"He said that he needs to be in Kolkata from Monday to Friday this week, and for that, would leave on Sunday night. He sent me the tickets and hotel stay confirmation email as usual. We always share travel documents with each other.

He left home at about 8, to reach the airport by 8:30 or so. The flight was at 10:30 PM. Since I am an early sleeper, I told him to message me after checking into his hotel in Kolkata. This morning, there was no message. I thought he might have forgotten, so I called him. The phone was switched off. He is in sales, he never switches off his phone. That's when I knew there was a problem. I called the hotel and they confirmed that there was a reservation, but he never showed up. I think that we should involve the police. It doesn't look ok." Latha completed.

"Yes," Shailesh agreed readily, "The police will have to be involved within the next hour or so. I want you to meet with someone from our security team. I have specially requested them to brief you on police procedures and your rights as a complainant. You should know a few things. It will be helpful. Do you have a lawyer?"

"Shailesh, you are not understanding. My first priority is finding Venkat. I am afraid that something might have happened to him. I think you should call up your Kolkata office and ask whoever he was supposed to meet. You usually send a car to meet your officers at the airport, no? Shouldn't that be the starting point?"

"Latha, I am sorry that I have to break this to you. Venkat was not going anywhere for an official visit. He was supposed to be in office. So, if he has sent you those tickets from his office id, with office id hotel reservations, that itself is an intent to... well, mis-inform. I don't think he is in any danger at all. There are certain other things that you don't need to know right now, but I will take the necessary approvals and try and share them with you by evening. Please meet the person from our security team. I am asking him to do this as a personal favour. After meeting him, you must go to the police station with Vandita and file a missing person's report. I can assure you, we are with you every step of the way. You have my number, call me anytime."

Vandita, Latha's friend, now understood why the company had insisted on having a female friend or relative present. Latha appeared to have entered a trance. She was looking at Shailesh as if he was a ghost. The colour had drained from her face and her eyes were glazed. As she made an effort to get up from the chair, Vandita placed a firm hand on her arm to keep her seated. Navita rushed to get a glass of water. Shailesh mumbled an apology of some sort and exited the room.

Navita and Vandita took care of Latha for the next few minutes. When she nodded that she was ready to meet the security team member, Navita brought him in. She was so, so sorry for this young lady. At that moment, more than anything in the world, she wished for Venkat to appear magically and face the music for his actions.

****

Navita sat through the briefing by the security team member. Afterwards, she went to Shailesh's cabin.

"When are you going to tell her about Afreen, boss?" she asked quietly.

"Is Afreen in office?"

"You know she is. That is the first thing we both checked. Also, she is appearing pretty perturbed, and she has asked me twice about Venkat. So, my guess is that she has no clue where Venkat is, either."

"You didn't answer her?"

"You know I cannot share the calendar of my bosses, boss." Navita smiled.

Navita assisted Shailesh, Venkat, and Gautam – three department heads.

Venkat reported to Shailesh but he handled the largest region – East. So, in terms of power, he had a lot. Gautam was the head of Legal for the company.

****

Latha came home by about 5 PM. Dejected and sore, she still kept dialling Venkat's number. She tried accessing his Google id to check his current location. The police, after knowing that her husband had sent her a bogus travel plan, had explained to her, nicely and gently, that her husband had vanished of his own free will, and she should try to get a lawyer, understand her rights, and secure whatever possessions she could. It was a sad occurrence, but not an infrequent one. Husbands and wives ran away all the time.

Vandita, her friend, was with her. She prepared dinner, ensured that they both ate, and then stayed back with her. When her husband called to ask how long she was planning on staying, she said, simply, "As long as it takes."

****

If it was possible, the next morning was even harder.

Shailesh and the legal head of the company, Gautam, came by to meet her.

"How are you feeling now, Latha?" Shailesh enquired gently.

"I am not better, but thank you for asking."

"We are following up with the police. We have some information from there, and some that we want to share with you ourselves."

"I think.. it's not good news?"

Gautam shook his head, "I'm afraid you're right. It's not. But the information from the police is positive. Venkat did check in; he did clear security. He simply did not board."

"So, he was at the airport, and then he just.. vanished? He was booked on a flight to Kolkata for sure, then?"

"And at the hotel, as you already know. You will be surprised to hear this, but we were not as shocked to know that he has vanished."

"Why?" Latha could not believe her ears.

"Latha, over the last year, Venkat has pocketed about 30 crores of sales proceeds that should have come to the company's accounts but somehow made it to third-party accounts that do not belong to the company. In short, officially, he was under investigation for embezzling 30 crores, but unofficially, we all knew he had done it. We were just trying to get the money back. The focus of the investigation was recovery, not prosecution."

"Venkat... did.. this? But... why?"

"When did he last take you on a holiday? And where?" Shailesh asked.

"To our temple town, with his parents. Last July." Latha answered, with some difficulty. Venkat was not a spendthrift kind of guy when it came to family.

"The ba^&*d." Shailesh muttered under his breath.

"Latha, you have only been married two years, I have known him longer. So, let me just say it out flat – Venkat was fond of the good lifestyle. He often fudged bills and took more money than he spent on company travels. But he was so good at his work that we simply looked the other way. He appeared to be this sincere, sweet guy, and he netted customers like nectar nets bees."

"So, you think he was a crook?"

"I KNOW he was a crook. It was only a matter of time. If he had refused to return the money, we would have filed criminal charges against him and then he would have had to see the inside walls of a prison." This was Gautam.

"But he is an only child. What will happen to his parents? He must have thought about that, surely?"

Gautam shook his head, "I think, you will find, Latha, that men like him rarely think about the impact on their family when they do these things."

"What do you think has happened?" Latha asked, "Please be brutally honest with me."

"I think that your husband has taken 30 crores and vanished into thin air, leaving you to deal with the mess and with his parents. You are the scapegoat, the fall guy, in this story." Gautam was as blunt as Latha had requested him to be.

"But you are helping me. Why?"

"Because not helping you would amount to helping a criminal. Helping you find him brings us closer to our 30 crores – an amount we cannot ignore."

"You think you can use me to get to him."

"No Latha, we are decent people. We will not use you as bait. Further, he would not have done this had he cared half a penny for you. We are just looking to work together."

That stung, but Latha knew it was true. Had Venkat cared at all, he would not have done this.

"Sure. Let's get him." Latha said with a new resolve in her voice.

It was at this point that Vandita stepped in, "So, we know what has happened, and we know why it has happened. I have been wondering, HOW did he do it? How did he vanish into thin air from the Mysuru airport?"

Shailesh looked at her sharply. Then he smiled. Vandita was going to be priceless.

****

A small taskforce was set up. Vandita, Latha, Shailesh, Gautam, and two other people – Amar, the head of Security, and Akash, the inspector assigned to the case. After the CEO of the company made a phone call and shared the 30 crores information, the police were quick to appoint an inspector level officer with 2 SIs (Sub Inspectors) to track down the 'missing person.'

The headquarters was established at Latha's house.

On hearing of Venkat's disappearance, his parents had come to Mysuru. When they heard what had happened, their worry shifted from their son to themselves, and the exit from scene was prompt.

It is funny how long a week can feel at certain times.

"It was Sunday night. He had to be on one of the flights. Check if he booked two flights on that day and flew on one of them. That would be easy enough to do." Amar was the first to speak.

"We have put his phone on surveillance. His debit card, credit card, his devices, Google id, everything is on surveillance. But so far, absolutely nothing." the inspector said.

"See, a guy cannot vanish in thin air. He has to deposit 30 crores somewhere. To collect the payments from our customers, he would have opened company accounts. Let's start by checking those. The customers who made payments into those accounts would have payee account details. Let's use that and find out who opened these accounts?"

"There were no wire transfers. All payment was taken in DD for these payouts. The DD could have been deposited anywhere in India. The payee's name was the same as this one." The SI informed.

"That is not possible. The Registrar of Companies will not allow two companies to open with the same name. It has to be a similar name. And, if a company has been registered in India, we know where to look." Gautam spoke up.

"Relax, Gautam. I am a CA. This is the easiest fraud in the world. The name of your company is personal. All he did was open a personal account with that name. And deposited money in it. Pay **Ashish and Co** is the same as pay **Ashish Company** to the average person. It could be absolutely anywhere in the country. Or it could be at many places." Vandita interjected.

"So, where can he be now?" Latha asked, yet again.

"I think I can answer that one." Amar spoke up. "Mr. Venkat Reddy and our money are safely outside this country, in a country with which India does not have an extradition treaty. At least a part of this money is in a crypto account somewhere. And we are not likely to hear from him again. I am sorry to say that his fraud may not be limited to 30 crores either. In the coming days, we are likely to hear from more customers about non-delivery of their products. We will then find out the true extent of his fraud.

I have spent the entire last week reading up about these financial frauds and how individuals do them. This, in short, is the playbook."

An expletive escaped Shailesh's lips.

"So, there is no point in looking for him, then?" Latha asked.

"There is always a point, Latha. He might think he has gotten away with this. But we are here – six people with six different types of expertise. I think, we can get him and make him pay. All we need to do is hang in there and not give up." Shailesh spoke up.

"We are going to be detectives now?" Amar asked.

"With all that you shared today, I think you already are." Latha replied, a shadow of a smile forming on her lips.

Another 3 days, nothing.

The task force was meeting frequently, in the hope that someone would hit something.

Today, Akash was the first to talk, "We have checked his Aadhar and identity documents against all international departures. No one has flown out with this Aadhar or passport. So, if he has flown out, he has done that on forged documents."

"Yes, but I don't think he has changed his name completely. When changing identity, criminals tend to retain some part of that former identity rather subconsciously. Venkat OR Reddy is there in some part of the new name. Find out about international fliers who have no previous history of flying outside the country and have a passport issued within the last 2 years." Amar contributed.

Akash made a note.

"Amar was right that day. The fraud is now at 40 crores and counting." Shailesh volunteered.

Latha spoke, "I am sure he is sending some money to his parents somehow. He used to be the only breadwinner. If we find where that money is coming from, we can find him."

Akash suggested something to Latha and she agreed to visit her in-laws the following morning. The village was only 4 hours outside Mysuru.

****

Two weeks had now passed. The team was meeting again. This was going slowly and painfully.

"You were right, Shailesh. Venkatgiri Naidu had a passport. It was issued 8 months ago, and his international departure was to Cyprus. Cyprus is one of the world's top centres for unnamed cash, and of course, crypto."

"Hmm, so he is in Cyprus. Can we find his crypto wallet?" Vandita asked.

No one knew how.

"Never mind, I will take care of that." She said cryptically.

"I have just come from meeting his parents. I told them that since he is a fugitive, his family will be roped in next. I need money to hire a lawyer. They tried to buy time saying they will arrange in a day or two, but I played the full emotional drama and mentioned urgency, and viola, came 2 lakhs to hire a good lawyer and keep them out of jail." Latha made her contribution.

"Hmm... that means that he is in touch with his parents for sure. They also seem to have enough money in the bank. Let me query their bank details. If the money is coming from an Indian account, we will at least get a lead." Akash interjected.

At the next meeting, Vandita held centre stage. "We found him! His money is with a crypto exchange called Coinbase. He is transacting from Cyprus, as we guessed. His current wallet size is only about 2 million USD. This is less than half the money he has taken from you. Which means that the rest of the money can either be in benami Indian accounts or in bank accounts in Cyprus."

It was time for Akash to contribute – "No Indian accounts. We checked. His parents are getting transfers from an international account only. Small sums at a time. So, he is transacting from where he is. We don't know how much he is spending. If his parents have 2 lakhs ready cash in their account, he is definitely not being thrifty."

"How did you get your information, Vandita?" Gautam was curious.

"Don't ask questions you don't want answers to, sir. Just that we freelance PIs (private investigators) have access to white hat skills that most institutions don't. Let's leave it at that." Vandita was simple and firm.

"So, in addition to being a CA, you are also a financial investigator?" Akash asked.

Vandita just smiled her assent.

Now, the team knew where he was, and where the money was. The next hurdle was to bring him to India without using the legal route. How could they make that happen?

****

Like a bunch of expert hunters, they laid a trap. Time was of the essence, because the next step for Venkat would be to call his parents over to join him. They had to place the bait before that. Once, he had to be convinced to return before the parents could fly the coup.

In this plan, the central role had to be played by Latha. Akash accompanied her to the village, where they pretended to have come to arrest the father. Latha played her part brilliantly, falling to the ground just as the father had to be taken away in the police car. Thus, she was stationed in the house.

Almost a month passed with no movement. Latha remained with her in-laws. The police dutifully came every third day and had to return because the father-in-law was needed to take care of the women in the house. The in-laws were grateful to Latha for falling ill when she did and took good care of her.

Not long after, Latha noticed some change in the demeanour of her in-laws. Her father-in-law was out of the house for 4-5 hours at a time. She knew that a movement was now imminent. Venkat was likely to come – either to Mysuru, or to the village itself. Mysuru airport and toll booths were on alert again.

One Thursday night, as Mr. Naidu got off his international flight, a police escort was waiting for him.

****

Venkat was sitting in the interrogation room, looking both angry and a little sullen. A lawyer had been summoned by and for him.

But the senior inspector in the room was an expert. He was from CBI, and Venkat was small fry.

"Welcome back," the inspector said gently. "Your lawyer will be here shortly, and then he can start emptying your pocket with his futile promises. Let me tell you how it will go. He will tell you that you are being sent to CBI remand and he will have you out on bail in 2-3 days at most. This circus will go on for 10 days, while he will charge you 2 lakhs per appearance for appearing in the CBI court on your behalf. After 10 days, your remand will pass to the police and the case to the court. From that point on, whether he charges 50k a hearing or 2 lakhs, is between you and him, but you, Mr. Venkat, are not going anywhere for the next 2 years. I promise you that. And once you cross the CBI remand home to the police remand home, you will find many examples to corroborate my theory. We know the law too, sir, and more importantly, we don't get paid per hearing. So, contrary to what you might believe, lengthening your trial is in your lawyer's interest and shortening it is in mine. Now, who do you want to listen to, to get out of this soup in record time?"

"What do you want?" Venkat hissed.

"A simple confession will do it. Anyway, you will spend many years in prison. The sooner you confess, the more lenient the judge will be. Take my word for it, or wait for about 100 court dates to figure this out. There will be no bail. Absconding is a non-bailable section. Like I said, we know the law too."

With that, Venkat crumbled, and the answers came quick and easy.

"How did you make it out of the airport?"

"I had a luggage loader's uniform in my hand baggage. I got out of the airport, left Mysuru by car, took a domestic flight from the nearest airport, and then boarded the international flight from Port Blair.

The rest, of course, you know. The money was already stashed in an offshore account in Cyprus and in crypto."

"Were 50 crores worth it?" asked the inspector.

Venkat shrugged. "Like you said, I am small fry. It was big enough for me."

"What were your future plans?"

This time, Venkat smiled before replying, "The usual. Stay in Cyprus, spend money, invest, live the good life, while you guys put Latha in jail, not willing to believe that she knew nothing about my scheme. I was not planning on calling my parents to join me, but your getting on my dad's case forced my hand. I had to come back to sign the village land sale papers once. Then, none of us would have touched down in India ever again. They would have flown out with me.

Unfortunately, I had no idea you had figured out my new identity. I thought you were just watching my parents and tracking their devices. So, all our communication was on Voice over IP[1]. I thought I was safe. Big mistake - underestimating you folks."

****

Outside, six people silently sat on a chai tapri[2], drinking tea. No one spoke, but there was a glint in each eye.

[1] A regular phone call can be monitored and text messages can be read by the telecom provider under an order from the police. But Voice over Internet Protocol – VoIP calls like Whatsapp calls, can neither be monitored by the police nor can these calls be tapped.

[2] A tapri is a makeshift stall for serving tea.

CHAPTER TWO

THE TAP THAT WATERS THE PLANT

"It's time, didi[1]." Anand opened her door gently and almost whispered.

She nodded and got up. Silently, but upright, she covered the distance from the room to the garden, where friends, family, and associates had gathered.

Her husband had made excellent arrangements. There was seating, cooling, refreshments, and a path for the mourners to follow. Some loyal staff from the house and office were working to manage the queue, unbidden. Grief binds people in strange ways.

She took her place in the pandal. The bhajans[2] went on for almost two hours. The pandal filled to capacity, then overflowed.

After the bhajans, the family mingled with close relatives. Friends and associates kept a respectful distance and helped themselves to tea and refreshments. This phase was not going to last long. 15 minutes tops. Then the first set of exits would begin and the family would have to take their place near the exit. Which is exactly what happened.

Du, Nishit, and the kids stood silently at the exit with folded hands. This part of the ritual was meant to thank everyone who showed up to share the family's grief.

Anand, who was a distant relative and house manager, stood on the other side, hands folded and eyes moist.

****

Durga, lovingly called Du, was the only child of Ramjas Chahal, the industrialist. Money is like blood - it attracts hounds and predators automatically. Ramjas, like most self-made industrialists, was watchful as a hawk and maintained his relationships in just the right way. Relatives were welcome to visit, but not to seek financial help. Friends were from similar financial strata, except old friends who were always welcome for most things. Take advantage of the man, however, and you had quite a different thing coming. Vidya, Du's mother, kept herself satisfied with unlimited money and no interest in the business. Du, on the other hand, was a natural and took to work like fish to water. Ramjas ji was a very proud father.

And then, Du had met Nishit. And fallen in love. So, Du and Nishit married, and Nishit came to live with them. At first, he made the pretence of looking for his own employment but within two years, merged himself into the company.

The household was completed by some staff that had been there for more than a decade – Bimla Tai, the de facto housekeeper, Suranjan, the cook, Amit, the only driver who could drive Ramjas ji's personal car, and Anand, the only family member who was trusted enough to be employed in the house. Anand was the house manager, confidante, and general doer-of-all-things-that-needed-doing.

Anand had come to the house as a young man, fresh out of Grade 12. Ramjas ji had hosted him for a while in the house while he did job hunting. Within that time, Ramjas ji recognised the talent of this boy and his inherent honesty. He offered Anand the role of house manager.

And now, 18 years later, Ramjas ji had passed away. Vidya ji was already gone. The next generation was in the saddle.

****

Barely six months later, Du attempted suicide out of grief. The loss of her only surviving parent, her mentor, and her everything, had been too much. She had tried therapy and other things, but it was just too much to bear. Her suicide note was emailed directly to the police, so that her family, and especially her children, would face no hardship because of her selfish action. She simply could not go on.

It was just that Constable Uday needed to buy bhajjis[3] from just that store, otherwise his mother-in-law would have fried him as well. And that was what saved Du. As soon as the police control room read the email, they immediately alerted all beats and one beat happened to be off route by as much as 5 kms (which in Mumbai traffic, is one hour) – but in the direction of Du's house. They were at Du's house in under 10 minutes and since emetic action is part of training, the police officers were able to revive her successfully. If touch-and-go had an illustration, this would be it.

As always happens in high-profile cases, Du vehemently denied that she had attempted suicide or sent that email. She even asked for the cyber cell to be involved. But the police are usually smarter. They did not believe her.

Nishit was also interrogated. But they found nothing to implicate him. If anything, he had been very mindful of his wife's grief. He had almost single-handedly taken over parenting full time. He had resigned from all work roles, leaving Du to manage things in the office as she pleased. He had accompanied her to therapy sessions, taken her out on holidays, and organized get-togethers with people she liked. He had confided to his friends, however, that his own struggles were going unaddressed. Though not as close as Du, he was also attached to his father-in-law, and having to deal with two losses – of his father-in-law and his wife as he knew her, coupled with the additional responsibility of being the full-time parent to one teenager and one 8-year-old – it was not easy on him. The police found out that as of last month, Nishit had also secretly started taking therapy.

The house staff was interrogated next. They all confirmed the same sequence of events. Ma'am was sad but not suicidal. Sir was just God's gift to Durga ma'am and the kids.

Bimla Tai, who had also taken care of Du as a child, was more tearful than the others. "I did not take care of even my own child the way I cared for Du beti. Seeing her like that was so heart-breaking, I wish I was lying there instead of her. May no mother have to see what I had to see that day."

Amit, who had taken to driving Durga didi now, was equally surprised. "She barely spoke after sahab[4] died. But when she did, she was confident and kind. No, sir, I don't think she would try to kill herself. Because she was aware of her duties – to the company, and I think, to her children. Besides, she was managing the business very well. Not at all like a person who does not want to, you know..."

Suranjan said that he had very little interaction with Durga ji, since Nishit bhaiya now took care of the household. He had nothing to contribute to the interrogation. Anand also maintained that Du didi now focused on work and barely interacted with him. He worked with Nishit.

Since nothing significant had happened to Du, the case was closed and filed. And that was that.

Until, September 2024. A good four months later.

This time, there was no suicide. Du just lost control of her car and it crashed. There were no survivors. Du was alone in the car. She crashed into the wall of a flyover. Bam!

Was Durga depressed? Her house staff, especially Bimla Tai, refuted that idea vehemently. She was definitely recovering. Maybe her medicines made her cocky and adventurous. Maybe that is why she accelerated from 60 to 100 within seconds.

Du's car was a luxury sports sedan that was all bells and whistles. It had the latest features inside and top-end safety features inside and outside. In a crash, the zillion air bags should have deployed and saved her. The accident proof frame protection should have ensured her safety. But they didn't.

The body was handed to the family after post-mortem and the police was about to close the case as an accident caused due to overspeeding, when one mischievous post on social media created a flutter – "What use are luxury cars if they can't save our lives?" said the post. It was made from an anonymous account.

Immediately, it was as if a floodgate had been opened. Hundreds of people reported lives lost in luxury cars when security features did not work as intended. The brand of car that Du was driving got special attention, of course.

This public clamour and the sheer number of cases made the Ministry sit up and take notice. India CEOs of all luxury brands were called and asked to demonstrate their safety features in crash tests to be conducted in India.

Obviously, this led to mayhem. International luxury carmakers do not demonstrate safety features to third world governments. Politely, but firmly, by the minister himself, no less, were these czars informed that if the crash tests were not demonstrated in Indian labs, their road safety certification would not be valid in India.

The carmakers asked for six months to comply with this requirement. After a very generous donation to the right funds, this request was approved.

****

And that is how the Durga Ramjas Death Case was officially reopened and handed to Rahul.

He was specially chosen for this case by the higher ups for very simple reasons – One, he loved cars. Two, he loved technology. He had put two unsuccessful applications for a vacancy in the national cybercrime team. Three, he was an IPS[5] officer, which meant that some level of gravitas and intelligence could be expected, and a CBI enquiry could be averted by the state police.

****

The case had to start from somewhere, so it started from the car. The airbags had not deployed. But why? The car manufacturing company said that this was because the car was traveling at a very high speed at the time of impact and therefore there wasn't enough time to deploy airbags. They also created illustrations to prove what happens in the event of a crash at such high speeds. The crash tests in labs are done at half that speed, they argued.

The illustrations soon made their way to social media and people started to argue about the human error component of this accident. Why speed on a road like this?

Rahul heard the luxury car maker. It took all his self-control to not burst out laughing.

"How is impact detected?"

"By a sensor on the outside – all around the frame, there are sensors. As soon as even one is activated, all air bags deploy immediately."

"Did the sensors fail this time?"

"No. The sensors must have detected the crash but the deployment takes 0.3 seconds, and we did not have that much time because of the speed."

"Then why can your cars go at that speed?"

"With all due respect, sir, following the speed rules of the country is the obligation of the driver."

"Hmmm... this is a connected car, no?"

"Yes sir, it is connected to the user's devices through Bluetooth. But unfortunately, that device was also destroyed in the crash. But the CCTV footage clearly shows how fast the car was going."

And that was that. The government increased the fines on rash driving all over the country.

Luxury car makers were asked to deploy speed jammers above the speed of 80. Politely but firmly, they declined.

****

God knows whether it was a desire to see the house that made him do it, or just idle curiosity. But Rahul made an appointment with Nishit to discuss the case at the latter's house. (Actually, it was neither curiosity nor desire. It was a solid suspicion.)

Nishit was very welcoming. He would have to invite his parents to stay with him soon, to take care of the kids, or send them to a hostel. Du used to take care of the office because she was so much better at it. But now, if he had to manage everything alone.... Well, it simply wasn't possible.

"Mr. Nishit, I am sorry, I have to ask – who inherits the wealth?"

"Well, there are three parts – me and the children. The children get everything that she got from her father. But I am the Trustee until they turn 18. I get some of her shares in companies. No one else gets anything significant. All the loyal members of the staff, and some extended family members get a few lakhs each."

"Are you much richer?"

"Not really. But even if I was, how would it matter? Have you seen my life? Would you wish this even upon an enemy?"

Rahul agreed that he would not.

Anand was invited to join them.

Anand mentioned that Durga didi was not like her father. She had inherited the same astute judgement about business, but not the wisdom of understanding people and their potential. "Durga didi would not have offered me the job of the house manager, for sure." Anand concluded.

"Was she polite and nice to the staff?" Rahul asked.

"Yes, she was. She was warm and kind. Just not a good judge of people. She sometimes hired people who were not the right fit for the culture of this household. Sometimes, she scolded the children unnecessarily. With Ramjas ji and Vidya ji, one of us, usually Bimla Tai, would save the children from the parents. But with Durga didi, you could not interfere when she was scolding. Even bhaiya could not always step in. So, in those ways, she was different. She was more... formula driven and less personal. Like Ramjas ji or Nishit bhaiya would get a gift for every member of the staff based on what we need in that year. But Durga didi would give me a budget and ask me to order the same thing for everyone. That was her style of working."

"Nishit ji, was Durga ji a rash driver?"

"She was a good driver. But whether she was going to be rash depended on her mood. Some days, she was. Some days, she wasn't. She loved this car and would not let anyone else touch it. Every weekend, she took this car for a spin. Sometimes we went together, usually she went alone."

"Like this time?"

"Like this time."

"Thank you for your time. I am sorry about the trouble caused by this social media post."

"At least it has told people that luxury cars cannot save their lives. Maybe they will drive more safely now." Nishit concluded as he opened the door for Rahul using a voice command on his smart home app.

"Oh wow! You have the full Adora Home Suite! How lovely!"

"Yes," Nishit smiled for the first time, "Anand got us to install this. He is the tech wizard in the house. He knows all about these latest things. He told me that I don't have to call the staff for simple things like drawing a curtain, raising the temperature of the room, or turning on the fan, etc. He takes care of most shopping, but I like to stock up on the girls' favourite things, school supplies, books, etc. myself. It is such a blessing since we installed it. This thing is being used in so many homes nowadays."

"That is true. Take Care." Rahul waved a bye on his way to the car. The meeting ended with almost a sense of friendliness. Camaraderie, at the very least.

****

Rahul knew he could (and should) close the case on negligent driving. But he didn't. He spent night after night on his laptop, reading and making notes.

The fatigue showed during the day, and within a week he was warned about his absentmindedness or lethargy. But the nightly research continued.

A week later, he made a progress report to his seniors. They approved his plan of action. The case was not going to be closed.

****

As in most investigations, speed was key. The warrants were delivered and assets seized on the same day. In fact, at the same time.

The cyber research office, Rahul's dream office, became his war room for 2-3 days. The guys here were really good. He was beginning to understand why he had been rejected. These guys were top notch.

At the end of the third day, they had their case.

All that remained now was a presentation and then one more warrant.

Rahul was apprehensive. "Is this conclusive? No doubt at all?"

Satyam, his SPOC[6] at the cyber unit patted his shoulder, "Relax, Tiger. We got this."

The presentation was made and the arrest warrant was immediately issued.

****

It took them two days, but then he cracked. The best way to disarm an educated culprit is to show him proof. That is what they did.

"I know how you did this. I just want to know why." Rahul said kindly when he knew the guy was going to crack.

"Oldest reason in the book, sir – money."

"You could have polished off a little bit at a time and no one would know. You don't even directly benefit from the will. Why do this at all? And why now?"

"See, I am not a thief. That is why Ramjas sir had given me the keys to the house. He also ensured that I remain well-watered. So, no greed. He had his money and I had mine. But his daughter had no tameez – no manners. She did not treat me like Ramjas ji and Vidya ji. And I did not want to steal. I am not a thief."

"But you are a murderer?"

"I will explain it to you like this. There is a tap and a plant near the tap. The tap gives out water which keeps the plant alive. Now, the plant does not want all the water of the tap. Only enough to keep his life going and growing. One day, the tap decides that it will not give any more water to the plant. Now, the plant can either die, or it can break the tap. If the plant is a survivor, what will it do?"

"How do you get money as a result of her death?"

"I don't get the money. My tap restarts. That is more important. And you have to remember, I did not expect to get suspected. Like, ever."

"That part is true. You are a genius. In the first case, you put the drug in her bitter morning drink, using her automated dispenser for the job. The email was a touch of perfection. But then, the police car reached in time to pump her out. No one believed her when she said she had not sent that email or attempted suicide. It was her IP, her id, her everything.

In the second case, you hacked the car. Durga did not crash the car. You did. From the house. The car company's servers tell us that they knew what had happened and had to stop the truth coming out no matter what. They didn't know WHO had done it. But they knew WHAT had been done. Where did you learn to code like that?"

"I just like coding. Why do you think I got Nishit bhaiya to invest in the full smart home solution? Did you know that most smart home solutions use open-source core? What is easier to hack than open-source code?"

Anand was charged.

****

Rahul and Satyam were preparing for their final debrief to their joint seniors.

"But Rahul..." Satyam looked up from his laptop.

"Yes?" Rahul responded.

"How did you know where to look?"

"The car companies told me."

Satyam: "Sorry?"

Rahul: "The diligence with which they hid the fact that this was a smart car, connected to their servers and all communication, including voice communication within the car, is backed up almost instantaneously on their servers. That's how I knew that this was a smart car crash. Then, it was just a matter of finding out who was tech savvy enough in her circle to do this and get away with it.

The rest, we did together – going over the recordings of all smart cameras, cloning smartphones, IP tracing, until we zeroed in on our hero man."

"Well, at least this time it's not the husband." Satyam shrugged.

"Thank God, Satyam. The kids need him." Rahul mentioned quietly.

[1] Didi means "elder sister" in some Indian languages. It is used to address a lady respectfully.

[2] Bhajan – a devotional song

[3] fritters

[4] Sir. Here, refers to Durga's father

[5] Indian Police Service – a national level service

[6] SPOC stands for Single Point of Contact. When we work with another organisation, usually that organisation assigns someone we can talk to for all our needs. This person is called the SPOC.

CHAPTER THREE

IT WAS ON THE NEWS

It was on the news. That is where she first heard it. "How?" She dialled his number immediately. It was picked up by HER. "Yes, he is really gone. Please don't come to the cremation." And with that, the phone was disconnected. For ever. For EVER. How permanent that sounded! And just 15 minutes ago, she would have laughed at anyone telling her that within the next 15 minutes, she would dial that number for the last time.

She sat down. Stunned.

He was ok last night. They chatted for a while, then he said he had to sleep, so she sent a 'Good Night' message and that was that.

He never woke up.

Tributes would pour in, of course. He was not the country's wealthiest start-up investor for nothing. He had invested in some of the companies that went on to become unicorns. He had made money, but more than that, he had created the one thing that start-ups were not able to create on their own – respect for start-ups.

In the heydays of 2000s, start-ups were outed as money guzzlers who created little or no value for their investors. At such a time, Vatsa had gone on stage at a national bankers' meeting and roared – *"Start-ups are not money guzzlers. The investors are idiots. They do not know how to pick the right start-ups and choose the right founders. Most of you have portfolios that show that 90% of start-ups fail. I am going to invest and create a portfolio where the failure rate is 10% and my capital growth will be in multiples, not percentages."*

Two decades and counting, he had come out on top and remained on top. He rejected 99 out of 100 proposals. But he caught the right ones with unfailing accuracy. Most of them went on to become profitable companies with stable managements and good corporate governance.

Today, he had died. Suddenly. According to the news channels, it was in his sleep. All she could do was stare at the news channels as they continued to update the details. She was never welcome in that house. And now, she would just never see him again. Not even to say the final goodbye.

She dialled his number once again. This time, his son picked up. "Rahul, listen to me, please. I just want to come and see him one last time. Will you please ask your mother and let me know? Just for one minute, I want to see him and touch his feet."

Rahul said nothing and hung up.

****

Supriya was the girlfriend that Vatsa never hid from the world. In every interview, he would refer to her as naturally as he referred to Rekha, his wife. Everyone knew her. And everyone also knew that she was never allowed to enter his house or interact with any member of the family. There were limits and they were scrupulously maintained.

30 minutes later, she got a call from his number. "Yes, please come. Do not touch his feet. You can say goodbye to him." was all Rahul said.

She changed into a simple pastel yellow salwar kurta and rushed to his house. Crowds were thronging the place – inside and outside.

She got off at the porch and made her way inside. Rekha was there. Vatsa was in a glass case, refrigerated. The viewing had a queue. She joined the queue and waited for her turn.

She saw him, bowed, and exited. Too numb to react. Too dead to think. Just.. saw him one last time.. and got out of there.

Back home, she started to think.

Sudden heart attacks happen all the time. She was sure of it. Yet, Vatsa was not the kind to go like this. He was too much of a lion, even at this age. And anyway, 60 is no age to go.

But foul play? For what? C'mon Supriya, you watch too many crime shows. Now you can't even let your boyfriend die in peace without thinking of foul play. Let it go!

But Supriya could not let it go.

She called her friend, the police commissioner, and asked for a post-mortem.

"Supriya, you're mad or what? You know how Vatsa lived! The good life, the late hours, they all add up, you know. If you want, I can talk to Dr. Iyer and get back to you, but what you are asking me to do is not possible. Please don't take his leaving so hard. You are losing your mind."

She agreed to get on a call with Dr. Iyer – Vatsa's long-time doctor and friend. He would have signed the death certificate for sure.

"Supriya... please don't worry. He died suddenly, but naturally. There is no foul play possible in a cardiac arrest. He died peacefully. That is our only blessing. Please put your fears to rest and try to come to terms with this colossal loss. Please surround yourself with friends. Take care."

Supriya noticed that Dr. Iyer did not end the chat with "We are all there for you."

'No,' she thought, 'that assurance is only for the wife.'
****

Supriya was surrounded by her friends. But that meant nothing. Vatsa and she had been together for more than 25 years. She had never married and was perfectly ok with that.

After the 13th day ceremony (which she could not have attended for obvious reasons), her friends tried to encourage her to step out of the house, even if for a short time. She politely requested them to leave her alone to deal with her grief.

On the 15th day, a phone call broke the silence of her now pointless existence.

"Supriya ji," it was Manikant, Vatsa's lawyer, "please come to our office at about 4 PM today. The will is about to be read, and I think you should be there. I have spoken to Rekha ji and she is ok with your presence."

"Thank you Manikant ji, but I have no interest in the reading of the will. It will only remind me, once again, that he is no more."

"Supriya ji," Manikant persisted, "I understand that you are financially independent and really don't need anything from Vatsa's estate. But please come. Trust me on this."

"OK." she quietly assented.

****

At the reading of the will, she discovered that she had got Vatsa's share in about eight investee companies. At current valuation, that made her rather rich. Of course, it was not a stitch on Rekha's fortune – both her own and what she got now from Vatsa. He had left everything else to Rekha, and the kids would only get anything at Rekha's passing. During her lifetime, Rekha was free to enjoy the dividends that came from the investments but was not allowed to transfer any assets to the children. She was free to make all other decisions related to the investments, and if the value of a single transaction crossed 100 crores, a designated Board of Trustees had to approve the transaction.

'Smart and foresighted as usual, sweetheart,' thought Supriya. Rekha was also a super sharp banker and had made her independent fortune in more traditional investments – she bought and sold stakes in publicly listed companies. They were a power couple for sure.

Once the formalities were over and the others were bonding over biscuits and tea, Supriya said her goodbyes and headed out. She was waiting by the lift when it happened. The lift was at a corner. This particular floor was not usually used, so there was no one else around.

"B^&(*rd! He already did it! I really thought we had it covered, Maya, but he had changed the will before sharing the intention with us! Now we can't get anything till mom's death. What a f^&*ed up b$%&*rd! I will never stop hating him!" That was the gentle, sweet, Rahul. He was presumably talking on the phone, because Supriya could only hear one voice.

Supriya smiled. She wasn't surprised. Vatsa was neither the first nor the last self-made millionaire to think that his children were useless wastrels who deserved nothing except hard work.

Rahul was obviously upset, but this conversation told her that Vatsa had shared the intention with his family. Ouch! Rahul and his sister, Veda, would have been upset, obviously! To not even get a penny on his death, and even their mother unable to help them! She felt even more sorry for them. They did not know yet what it meant to lose a father. In the months to come, they were going to find out.

But then she remembered that both kids already owned some equity in his family office, where all dividends were consolidated. So, for sure, their living expenses would be taken care of.

Without realising it, she heaved a sigh of relief. She had seen these kids grow up through Vatsa's conversations, and she cared.

****

It was a warm summer day when Rekha's phone rang. She didn't recognise the number.

"Yes?"

"Rekha, this is Supriya. I would like to meet you please."

Rekha's first instinct was to slam the phone. She had too much on her plate right now to be nice to the mistress of her insensitive, mean ex-husband, who never paid her the attention that she deserved and craved.

But then, curiosity took over, "Why do you want to meet me?"

"Will tell you when we meet. The Savoy, please. We'll book a suite to talk. It is not a good idea to be seen meeting in public. Just name the date and time. And you can walk out if you don't like the chat. Promise."

"Ok." And Rekha hung up.

****

On the appointed day, Rekha and Supriya made their way to separate entrances, used the special private elevator, and were shown into the suite.

Rekha sat down. Supriya handed her an orange juice.

For some weird reason, in the privacy of this room, Rekha felt relaxed. Perhaps for the first time since Vatsa, she felt no animosity towards Supriya. She realised just how good it was to not be in the public or private eye. To be the judge, not the judged. Oh, that felt good! Even better than the weekly spa that she forced herself to take.

Supriya was attentive without being intrusive.

At her own pace, Rekha spoke.

"So, tell me."

Supriya came and sat in front of her. Looked her straight in the eye. And then said, softly, "Rekha, please tell me what's going on. Something is not right. I can sense it in you. Please talk to me. You and I are the only ones who really understand what we have lost."

Rekha smiled mirthlessly. "Speak for yourself, my dear. His love was all yours."

"No. You know that. He loved us both. But more importantly, we both loved him. Even if we didn't lose the man who loved us, we have both lost the man we loved. Only we can know what it's like to lose him."

"Yes." Rekha's voice dropped to a whisper, "But why are you asking me this? Why care?"

"I saw your pictures from the FICCI event. You don't look right. I don't know why I called. It was just a strong hunch."

"Hmm." Rekha was quiet for a while, "And if I tell you, you will start blackmailing me." She said matter-of-factly.

Supriya visibly recoiled. As if she had been stung.

Then, regaining her calm, she continued, "Rekha, my dear, you have to know this. I already know enough about your life to blackmail you, if that is what I wanted. After Vatsa, as many as three publications offered me mindboggling numbers as "advance" for doing a sleazy tell-all on our relationship. So, sweetheart, I think, you must understand, that even if I am not 5% of your net worth, I am a worthy person."

Rekha looked down and bit her lip.

For a few minutes, there was silence. Supriya contemplated leaving but didn't.

"It's my health. I don't know what it is. But I never feel well. Rahul and Veda got a full body check-up done and I was diagnosed with hypertension. Dr. Iyer prescribed some mild medicine but even taking that makes me giddy. So, I throw the pill away and lie about having taken it. But I know hypertension is a silent killer and I should be regular with the medicine.

"Do you have any symptoms of hypertension?"

"I had palpitations many times after Vatsa passed away. At first, I thought it was grief. But when months passed and things didn't get better, Rahul and Veda took me to Dr. Iyer. I am now their only parent. For their sake, I want to live long."

"Hmm." Supriya thought for a moment, "OK, so this is what you are going to do. You will go to Delhi for a work meeting. There, you will complain of poor health and stay back for 1-2 days. This time, you will spend with me. I have a villa there that is away from the media glare. Let's get you a second opinion. Maybe it's just a matter of changing your hypertension medicine."

Rekha agreed. More, perhaps, for the break than anything else.

****

The Delhi visit was a stupendous success. Rekha got a second health check done and was found to be absolutely fit and fine. On the way back to Supriya's villa, she could not control her enthusiasm. "The kids will be so happy! Thank you for doing this, Supriya! I am very grateful to you. We have all been so stressed over my health. I can almost see their grins right now."

"Errm.. Rekha?"

"Haan?"

"Agar na batayein to[1]?"

Rekha's eyes widened in disbelief, "Arre!? Kyun[2]? They will be so happy."

"Socho na[3], What if we don't tell them? As a game? Keep-a-secret types?"

"Baba[4] first they will drive me nuts over that medicine."

"No. Tell them you are taking it, but throw the medicine."

"You have something on your mind, Supriya, but if it involves fooling my kids, I won't have it and I won't let you do it. We have just taken a 3-day trip. We are not BFF[5]s." Rekha was stern.

"You are right. It's not against your kids. It's for you. Please just don't tell anyone right now?"

"OK.."

"And one more thing. For your safety, please ensure that you go to the kitchen and serve yourself for the next few days."

Rekha gasped, "Are you seriously insinuating that someone on my staff is poisoning me? How well do you know them? They've been around for years!"

Supriya maintained her calm, "Rekha, right now, all I know is that your husband died suddenly of a heart attack. Within a few months of his death, you, who have always had radiant skin and a tall bearing, have dark circles under your eyes and look visibly unwell. A lot of it is grief. But it is worth checking out that there is nothing more. Can you trust me on this?"

"Why would you do this?"

"You may find this strange, but I care. I care for everything that he held dear, and you."

For the first time, Rekha nodded, almost imperceptibly.
****

Supriya was not someone to tread lightly. She worked like a duck – calm on the surface but kicking furiously underneath. It took her just a few weeks to get things sorted.

It was time to meet Rekha again. But this time, not just Rekha.
****

On the appointed day, Supriya was beyond herself. There were palpitations and anxiety and what not. A private security person was serving coffee in the suite that had been booked for her get-together.

Rekha was the first to arrive. Supriya hugged her real tight. If Rekha was surprised, she didn't show it.

Dr. Iyer was next. Then Rahul and Veda turned up together.

It was time to begin. If Supriya felt a little like Poirot, she didn't show it.

"Rahul beta, it must have been very disappointing for you, no[6], to not get anything when your dad passed away. I would have been very angry in your place." Supriya was sounding like the aunty making polite conversation.

"Supriya, please, you are not my buddy. Or anyone's. Nor are we here to discuss my dad. You called us for a clarification related to dad's will. Where is the lawyer?"

"The lawyer, my dear, has a name – Manikant ji. He is delayed. And what I am about to do is going to help you, so if I were you, I would be polite and nice. Under the will, your mother cannot transfer any assets to you. But that restriction does not apply to what I got from your dad."

Rahul's eyes widened. His body language changed. Immediately.

"So sorry for misunderstanding you." He almost stammered.

"Your mother and I have used this time to develop a careful friendship. Both of us feel that you kids, being mature adults, should be given assets to manage. So, I am transferring a quarter of what came to me under Vatsa's will to you, and a quarter to Veda. In short, you guys are getting half my inherited fortune."

"Are you giving something to me also, ma'am? Otherwise, I am not sure why I am here. I was told you wanted to discuss Rekha's health?" This was Dr. Iyer.

"Sorry, Dr. Iyer, you have been invited to discuss Rekha's health only." Supriya smiled, "We are going to make this quick. And I would like you to know that I already know the answers to the questions I am about to ask. Why is Rekha on hypertension pills?"

Dr. Iyer's eyes widened, but only for a split second. "Because she is hypertensive. Since Vatsa's death."

"No sir, she is not. And you know it."

"Madam, I hope you know what you are talking about. I have my BP[7] meter in my kit. Let me prove a few things to you right now."

"But right now, she has taken your medicine. So, her BP would be normal, right?"

"Yes."

"Sure, let's verify that then. I have a BP Meter right here. Not as good as yours. This one is automated." Without waiting for an answer, Supriya went and checked Rekha's BP.

"There, it's normal." Dr. Iyer almost screamed as soon as the machine beeped and showed its numbers.

"Exactly." Supriya said calmly, "She is not, and has not been, on your medication for many weeks now. And yet, her BP is absolutely fine. So, Dr. Iyer, I ask you, again, why has medicine for hypertension been prescribed to her?"

Dr. Iyer was not an idiot. He immediately congratulated Rekha on regaining her health on account of her positive attitude and started to leave. At which point, the coffee server politely handed him a coffee while blocking the entrance to the suite.

"And now, Rahul and Veda, maybe you want to confess to your mom? I can assure you, I know all the answers. The only reason you guys are here is so you can tell your mother yourselves. She does not know yet, and I don't want to be the one to tell her."

Rekha couldn't hold herself any longer, "What? Are you really accusing my kids of being a part of this? I beg you, Supriya, even if this is true, I do not want to know. Dr. Iyer has been the custodian of our health for many years. That is betrayal enough. If my children are also involved, what do I have to live for? If my own children want me dead....." and here she paused, unable to continue.

Rahul and Veda sat down on either side of Rekha. They started talking – very, very slowly. There wasn't that much to tell. The plan was simple. Dr. Iyer had approached Rahul and Veda after he got to know about the will. He offered to prescribe hypertension medication to Rekha. This would give her hypotension – low BP, for which there is no medicine, but which is more dangerous than hypertension.

Then, one fine day, Dr. Iyer would conveniently find that her BP was dangerously high and give the medicine intravenously.

She, too, would pass peacefully in her sleep, with a medical certificate signed by a very rich and powerful Dr. Iyer. No one would think to check since months of prescriptions would establish the presence of hypertension and her going in sleep would be written down to a silent heart attack. It was so simple it was pure genius. Dr. Iyer would be rich for the rest of his life with money on a tap from the heirs, and so long as they paid, their secret would be safe with him.

After the confession, Rekha spent some time alone with her children. Then, they were taken to another room.

Rekha sat in a chair, in shock. "My children? My own children! Agreed to a plan like this?"

"Relax, Rekha. The important thing is, we stopped this in time. Right now, in that other room, a lawyer is telling them the worst thing that could have happened to them today. I don't think your kids love money enough to go to jail. So, likely, this is the end of the episode. They thought they could be smart. I had to show them they were being dumb."

"But how did you know what you knew?"

"Oh, the oldest trick in the book! I put spyware on their phones. Our young people are rather disrespectful of security and very trusting of random videos received for entertainment."

"Why did you suspect?"

"That one is simple too. Those black circles under your eyes at the FICCI event indicated that something was going wrong rapidly. The Delhi clean chit meant that someone was giving you something to make you sick. Since the only medicine they started for you was the hypertension one, the rest was a simple web search."

Rekha was stunned. At long last, she managed a 'Thank you' and a hug.

[1] What if we don't tell them?

[2] Kyun - Why

[3] Think about it

[4] Baba is a generic term used to address another person.

[5] BFF – Best Friends Forever

[6] This 'no' is used in Indian English to denote Isn't that so?

[7] Blood Pressure

CHAPTER FOUR

THE DIARY OF AMIT SHARMA

"Will he be here today?"

"Yes, he is arriving by the afternoon flight. Be ready."

Inspector Sharma blew on his cigarette, then let out a deep sigh and a ring of smoke. 'Smoking is so uncool and unhealthy', he thought, then took another puff, 'But it's the best at-work de-stressor.'

Sharma was the king of Saam-Daam-Dand-Bhed[1] – any means to get one's work done. He also specialised in bringing big criminals down. He was summoned by the CBI whenever they needed help.

In his home jurisdiction, of course, the criminals had a Brahmastra[2] that he could not counter – money and its power over his superiors. Therefore, out of respect to the Hindi proverb – in a flowing river, all must wash their hands, he used to help himself to his fair share of the proceeds. Even though it was his hard work that gave his superiors the power to command a higher price from their stakeholders, he would get only the fair share according to his rank. And, to ensure that he does not step on their toes, he was also rewarded with an oral warning from time to time.

But at the CBI office, he was a completely different man. Agile, alert, and observant, he paid attention to every piece of paper, every photograph, every text message. Like a hawk, he watched the suspects and the surveillance videos. He read the autopsy reports like a vulture – getting every ounce of detection that he could out of them. Here, if anywhere, was his genius put to any good use.

But today, even at the CBI office, he was stressed. Amit was due to arrive by the afternoon flight.

****

The story started two weeks ago. Inspector Sudhakar Sharma was travelling his regular route – Delhi to Bareilly. The passenger in the next seat was an interesting man. Sharma had an instinct about these things. He started a conversation and found soon enough that as usual, he had been right. The man on his left was a cyber sleuth – someone who uses internet technology to catch hackers and other general range cyber criminals. He worked with private corporate clients and occasionally with the cyber police.

Sometime during the short flight, Sharma said, "I am sure you can catch your cyber criminals using technology and hacking easily. But in my field, it is different. We have to use on-ground methods to nab our on-ground criminals. These guys kill for money, do drugs business, hawala, arrange high-end bribes and kidnappings.. it's a messy, bloody business."

Amit, the cyber sleuth, was silent for a bit. "What if we place a bet? My techniques do not just help with cybercrime. They can help you nab your criminals too."

"But Amit, we know our criminals. We send our juniors to be deployed as security guards in their palatial houses. We just don't get the proofs."

Amit was silent for a while.

"I have a plan. I have been playing with it for a while. Maybe it is time for us to work together."

"How so?"

"I think technology can be used to do old-fashioned sleuthing."

"Oh God, Amit ji, you think we have not tried to put mics and cameras in their houses? Of course, we have! It doesn't work! They get to see the camera and the mic. We have been beaten over that method so much that we don't even want to try it anymore."

"But you see, sir, that is the difference. This time, they will be the ones putting the cameras and the microphones. They will make the cameras and the microphones follow them everywhere. We just have to be present at the collection point."

Amit had Sharma's attention.

****

A plan was hatched and Sharma spoke to his seniors at CBI. They could not believe what they were hearing. "This is not possible."

"I think it's worth a shot, sir. At least one city. But no local police involvement. If we can help even one innocent victim, it will be worth it."

The matter had reached the CBI Director, no less. He sat on the proposal for two days. Then, he called Sharma and his CBI sponsor, Nandu, directly.

"Nandu, tell everyone that the proposal has been rejected. After that, I never want to hear it mentioned. I am making a special team of exactly three people – you, Sharma, and this guy Amit. You will work out of Amit's office. No government building.

Your on-ground action force will be a 15-member special commando team. They will work in civvies. We are not an action team. We are an investigative agency. I am taking the funds out of my discretionary account. We won't pay Amit anything and you, Sharma, will be on deputation without deputation fee. Is that ok for you? You will survive on your base salary only. Nandu, you will have to multitask AND hide the existence of this task force from your colleagues, team members, and family.

I am giving you six months. Prevent two financial frauds, save six lives, or get evidence for some cases that the CBI is not able to otherwise prosecute. Do anything. I don't care. Get me results.

And then, we will see."

Never had two men walked out of the CBI Director's office with grins wider than these two men that day.

Amit was called. He was equally thrilled.

The team moved quickly. The on-ground force was trained at a private location, donated generously by one of Amit's corporate clients who owed Amit some hefty consulting fee and was happy to get away with the use of the facility instead.

The equipment was procured. The plan was set in motion.

Four months later, the CBI Director went for an evening walk and strolled into Amit's office.

****

A week later, the CBI interrogation room:

A bewildered man sat in a chair in a room that had three cushioned chairs, one table, an earthen pot full of drinking water, a steel tumbler, and nothing else.

The room had a window that looked out into the garden.

Nandu played the audio recording from his phone. The CBI Director was in the adjoining room, watching and listening through the monitor.

The other man heard, incredulous. His eyes growing wider with each word.

"You cannot use that in court."

"There won't be a court because there won't be a kidnapping, my dear sir. If you think that even after having this information, we will let carry out this plan, you are sadly mistaken. We know we cannot prosecute, but we can prevent. We are convincing you to do that. You could, of course, decline. But, the child is already in a safe location. You, on the other hand, will have to suffer unnecessary loss if you even try."

"But... how did you get this recording? It is illegal. If I find one illegal mic embedded in my house, you will have hell to pay."

"Be our guest."

****

And that, was the first of about ten meetings that Nandu had in the next three months. Each time, a crime was prevented by bringing in the person and telling them that the crime was not viable anymore. Sometimes, the victims were saved without telling anyone anything. Sometimes, the trained force would be present "by chance" at a crime spot when the criminals arrived. Dressed in civil clothes, they acted as 'vigilant citizens' and prevented the crime by sheer physical training – for which the local gang peer training was no match.

At the end of the sixth month, the CBI Director, Amit, Nandu, and Sharma were in Amit's office. Ostensibly, this was a performance review. But everyone knew the secret program had passed with flying colours.

"Amit, Sharma, Nandu – in the last 3 months, you guys have prevented fifteen kidnappings. You have also averted two bomb blasts and saved twenty potential murder victims. I am astounded.

You have to tell me how this worked."

Amit spoke.

"Sir, first, let me tell you that I am very grateful to you for giving us this chance. Using technology to prevent crime rather than detect it, has been on my mind for a long time. You, Sharma ji, and Nandu ji - you trusted my idea and gave it a chance. So, thank you.

Secondly, this program, successful as it has been, possibly cannot be replicated nationwide or even put into an institution. But I think it can be used in a limited way under exceptional circumstances.

I will now tell you what we have done. Let's start from there. I don't know the legal process, Nandu and Sharma are the experts on that. I only know how to use tech to pre-empt crime. I had been working on that theory for almost a year when Inspector Sharma and I met on that flight.

There is one company that readily enters your house, knows what you watch on TV, what you buy, where you live, what your house looks like, and everything that you say. All of this information rests with this one company. Fortunately for us, that one company also has one of the world's largest cloud storage solutions, where this data is stored, and the security of that cloud storage solution is weak enough for many of its clients to lose their data stored on its servers.

This company also employs humans to listen in to conversations that its clients have in their homes. Presumably, the objective is to understand whether its home assistant is saying anything offensive, and to improve the response of the AI led home assistant. In such a scenario, all we needed to do was creating a backdoor entry to access the audio recordings of this device. Then, we change the device settings to record all audio in the ambient conditions. Most people will put this AI home manager in all their rooms. So, it doesn't matter where they are discussing the plan or even if they walk while discussing the plan. The audio recording device is everywhere.

The same company also owns the company that makes connected AI robotic vacuum cleaners. This was the best part of our strategy, to get visuals by hacking the connection of the robotic vacuum cleaners to the servers of the company. The customer gives consent to the company to store information about their house on their servers so that their robotic vacuum cleaner can learn from this data and clean the house more efficiently. The device can be controlled through an app. Now, the app can be on any device, including ours. So, we use that.

The third element was to understand the daily routine of the family members we were interested in. We then had to set our activities to do targeted listening. As a resource crunched team, we trained our program to listen in and tell us the highest volume time of day. We even trained it to listen for some key words that are related to the trade. At that time, we acted as the human listeners and also programmed the vacuum cleaner to be present in the room. The vacuum cleaner is so silent you won't even notice it. But it can get us visuals of the people present in the room. It has a fantastic HD camera and sensor to help it clean better.

We did not do any snooping. Nor did we install any snooping devices or mics in the houses. That is why they could not find anything. We just added one more collection pipe for the data already being collected.

With this, the special team trained by Sharma sir and Nandu sir was able to take pre-emptive action to take the potential victims to safety before the event could take place. In some cases, we were also able to install a decoy and catch the field workers while they were attempting the murder. But those are small fry field workers. The biggest satisfaction is that we were able to prevent crime, and the gangsters have no idea how."

"How did you put the devices in their houses? Was it spray and pray?"

"Yes sir, in part, and in part, surgical strike. We specifically targeted the young users of these families and then used the network effect as their social circle installed the devices one by one. That is why the first four months were so slow. We got about 70% conversion, which was brilliant. We would have been lucky with 50-55%."

"But we cannot institutionalize it, can we? It's a privacy nightmare." The CBI Director intoned.

"Yes sir. Unfortunately, when you try to use this information to prevent crime, it's a privacy nightmare. Our citizens will willingly give their data to a large company, but if we even create a conduit to get a part of that data for an automated crime prevention program, with fewer human listeners than the private company, they will not allow it.

Further, if we, as private citizens can do it, criminals can also do it to do the exact opposite thing. Imagine having this information about a victim you want to kidnap or kill." Amit resigned.

"But, sir, there must be SOMETHING we can do with this brilliant process! We can infiltrate the entire crime network using the infrastructure put in place by a global company!" Sharma interjected.

The CBI Director was quiet for a very long time. Finally, he spoke, "No, we cannot do it. The privacy angle is a valid concern.

Sharma, Amit, I understand your anguish at having something so brilliant but not being able to use it. But remember, our people are people first. We cannot take their privacy away in the name of protection. That is what a police state does. We are not a police state.

Amit, I am also mindful of the other thing you said – if we, as private citizens could do this so easily, the criminals will be two steps ahead of us. We must take steps to ensure that our state secret data does not travel through the same conduit. That is the second important takeaway for me. Not just what we can do to others, but also what criminals can do to us.

We can keep the team in place. You three will remain in touch. We will have to disband the commandoes. But when the air in a particular city gets warm, I will call upon you guys to help us prevent mass human incidents. I know your incubation time is four months. Try and see if you can shorten it. I am approving one more pilot. This is the name of the city. Give me two months of incubation."

Then, he stepped out. At the door, he turned and said, "Congratulations, guys! There are people out there who owe their lives to you today. And they will never know it. Amit, proud of you! Sharma, thank you! Nandu, well done!"

With that, the CBI director went home.

****

Next week, there was a meeting in the Home Ministry.

At 5 PM, the Home Ministry released a directive for all ministers, Members of Parliament, judiciary, Central Government employees, personnel and key vendors of the Indian Armed Forces, paramilitary forces, and all personnel and ranks.

The Directive forbade the use of the connected AI devices in the homes and offices of the personnel. Violation at home was to be punished with internal disciplinary action and violation in office was to be punished with strict criminal charges. The list of forbidden devices included inane articles like AI home assistants and even robotic vacuum cleaners!

Everyone was flabbergasted.

News channels scrambled to get "experts" to talk about the Draconian measures being put in place by the fascist government. Anyone who was anyone was on a TV channel, talking about personal rights in the house and how the government will no longer be an employer of choice. Reservations in government jobs were brought up, bureaucracy was cursed, ministers were cursed. The technophobia of the cowherd politicians received special attention too. "What about employee privacy?" was the overarching theme of the TV debates.

The morning papers screamed: "Technophobic Government bans modern technology".

In his house, Amit smiled genially, folded the paper, and gently placed his coffee cup on the tray.

[1] Saam-Daam-Dand-Bhed is an Indian strategy for winning a negotiation. Saam – Explain your point of view to the person and convince them. Daam – Bribe them or give financial incentive. Dand – Threaten them with dire consequences, Bhed – If all else fails, find out a secret from their life and blackmail them with it. The strategies are to be used in order – the subsequent strategy employed only if the previous ones fail.

[2] A celestial weapon that never fails. Used metaphorically here to mean a super power.

THE DAY DHANI DIED

"It looks all wrong."

This is how a murder-dressed-as-suicide case begins in Marple[1]'s head. But in Sharad's case (that's me, by the way), this is how it looked destined to end.

I did not know that it was a murder-dressed-as-suicide. I did not know whether it was a murder, suicide, or accident. I did not like crime capers. Or crime anything. But here I was, the absolute central figure of a death. Because that was the only certainty – there had been a death, and I was the central figure in the story of that death, simply because, I was, through some societal law, deemed to be the central figure in that life.

My wife was dead.

I was not the central figure in her life. Just like I have never been the central figure in my parents' lives. Or in anyone else's life. No, that's not true. I was the central figure, even if briefly, in the life of Vatsala. But that was so long ago. And for such a short time. Never before, and never since, have I been the central figure. I have no experience in being a central figure. Why could they not choose someone more experienced?

But the police had chosen me. On the basis of statistics (because nothing else was handy). Most wives were murdered by their husbands. And of course, the hatred of my in-laws.

The hatred of my in-laws was the overarching theme of my family life.

It had started innocuously enough. The mother's daily phone calls to the daughter after her marriage. Dad used to join in too. I found them so cute and so affectionate. My parents never found time to call me and talk every day.

Then one day, Dhani suggested that we look at a house in Ganga Colony to buy.

"To buy?" I asked incredulously, "But we don't have that kind of money!"

"But we can always get a loan, na! Dad says that home loans are really cheap and this is a great way to build real estate assets early in life."

I could not put a finger on why that made me feel uncomfortable. So, I discussed it with a friend, and thought a lot more.

Finally, I came to my bride of less than two months, took her hand in mine, and said, softly, "My sweetheart, we really should build assets together and secure our future. But what to invest in, where to buy, when to buy, and how to fund it, should be a decision made by you and me, not influenced by anyone else."

I thought I had rehearsed it well. I thought it would help her see a future in which both of us were joint decision makers.

I was so wrong. So, so wrong.

That conversation started the downward spiral of my relationship with my wife, and the hatred of my in-laws. It wasn't hatred at first, just irritation at my being this obstinate, unaware fellow. The hatred, I think, grew slowly, but steadily, fuelled by big and small incidents. Like the time when Dhani asked me to join them all for a family dinner at her parents' place on a Friday night, to welcome another son-in-law from the extended family. I hadn't wanted to go but tagged along. And for an inexplicable reason, developed the mother of all migraines, spoiling the dinner for everyone else.

But all that was in the past. Compared to my problems today, those memories were laughable. Cute, even.

Today, I was being accused of murder.

The SI[2] was the seniormost member of the team that came to the house. Usually, when someone dies in their sleep, people don't call the police. But those are normal people. Not the parents-of-Dhani-who-hate-Sharad. When I returned from my business trip and found Dhani dead in her bed, I informed my parents first and her parents right after.

I expected everyone to come together to grieve. But what happened next took me completely by surprise. Within 15 minutes, the police were at the door. They took charge of the situation immediately, and my father-in-law, shortly after. The SI asked me a lot of questions, checked my boarding card, asked me why I took the morning flight home, instead of the night one, as most people returning home do, and sent the body for post-mortem. Losing Dhani was bad enough, but subjecting her body to post-mortem, or losing my freedom... that was ... beyond belief.

I was taken to the police station, where a more senior Inspector took charge. He was slightly softer. Offered me tea. I was in a daze. My father and brother were waiting outside the Inspector's cabin. A lawyer was on his way. No, no, no, this was all wrong. Dhani gone, handcuffs instead of a shroud, me, a widower, or worse still, labelled a murderer.

"Why did you take the morning flight?"

"I had a dinner to attend. Morning flight was the only choice."

The Inspector nodded.

"How do you think she died?"

"I have no idea! She is so young! How can she die?"

He nodded again.

"How come no one missed her all morning? No newspaper wala, no milkman, no morning maid? No one called at your house?"

I smiled, in spite of myself. "We don't get the newspaper at home, sir, and milk we buy when we need. Usually, she picks it up on her evening walk. There is no morning maid because Dhani is not a morning person. She rarely wakes up before 11:30-12:00 noon. Then, she calls up the maid and she comes to do the work."

This time, he didn't nod. His eyebrows arched, if ever so slightly.

"That's certainly....different. Must have inconvenienced you a lot, your wife sleeping in late every morning?"

My surprise was genuine, "Why should it inconvenience me?"

"Well, you know, who will send you to the office and all?"

"I am not a child, sir." I said that, hopefully, without sounding rude.

But the Inspector judging my dead wife and treating me like an invalid in the same sentence, was just a little bit irritating.

"Hmmm. ... The post-mortem report will be here soon. But see, Mr. Sharad, it's something we deal with every day. The thing that works best, I can tell you from 20 years of experience, is if the person comes clean. The sooner the better. Your in-laws look like bullies. We want to help you. Your father-in-law, unfortunately, has reach. So, the case will not remain with me for long. I can only help you in a short window, maybe as short as two hours. Tell me what happened, and I will bring your lawyer in, we will work out the loophole that will save you, and you can send a small token of gratitude to my house later."

"You don't understand. I wasn't in town. And I have come clean. I opened the door with my key, opened the door to my bedroom, and figured out as soon as I touched her that she was gone. I felt giddy immediately and came out of the room. Then, I opened the windows because suddenly, the air was stuffy. Then, I called dad. That's it."

"Hmm. You know, I believe you. There is henpecked and there is in-laws pecked. You are the latter. Was your wife a sweet person? Or was she like her parents?"

"I loved her." Was all I could say. And it was true.

"You are using the past tense already." The inspector said meaningfully.

After that, there was no conversation.

My lawyer came and showed some papers to the police. I had no idea what was going on.

The two warring families were outside. I stepped out of the inspector's cabin and was immediately surrounded by my family like a protective shield. They whisked me away even as my father-in-law (now, ex-father-in-law) started screaming profanities.

At home, we all sat. They heard me out. Then, we consulted with the lawyer. He had only one advice for me – get all your paperwork in order - your tickets, your hotel stay, who you were with, and make sure the entire story is TRUE.

"But it is!" I protested again.

The police came back to our house. They entered the sealed room and started looking.

After a while, they came out with an object.

"Did you always use it in the room?"

"No. This was for use in the balcony. I told her to not bring it inside."

"Why did you tell her to not bring it inside?"

"The coal burns and leaves tiny black soot particles all over. Besides, this is not safe for indoor use."

"Did your wife share that view?"

I smiled mirthlessly. If Dhani were alive, that smile would have been sardonic. But she was dead, and my smile had no meaning anymore.

"My wife did not share any of my views."

"Did you bring this inside?"

"No. I would never bring that inside."

"Could she carry this herself, without help?"

"When it is not full, sure she can. The frame is not very heavy, as you can see for yourself."

"Hmmm."

My in-laws were not permitted inside the building by the police, but they were waiting downstairs. The Inspector who had met me at the station was with the team that came. He invited them upstairs.

They came up, full of bridled fury that would remind one of a simmering volcano. We did not look at each other.

"Mrs. and Mr. Bose, do you recognise this? Where did this come from?"

Mrs. Bose was the first to speak. "I gave this to my daughter as a gift. So fond of this she was. Was she murdered with this? How ghastly! I am sure you found the impact wound."

The inspector raised a hand. She shut up.

Everyone was then signalled to sit down.

"Mrs. Bose, did you talk to your daughter last night?"

"Yes, yes, like every night. We spoke for a long time!"

"What did you talk about?"

"The usual, her house, her life, and.. <here she paused> her usually absent husband."

"Did you discuss this object?"

"Yes! She told me how warm and cosy it makes her feel and how this boy hates her even getting such simple pleasures of life. She wants to carry this with her wherever she sits and he won't let her! Small particles of soot are more important to him than my daughter's happiness!"

The inspector said nothing for a minute. He just looked down at his shoes, and then spoke - deliberately, confidently.

"Mrs. and Mr. Bose, Mr. Sharad, and... the entire family, all of you, I have something important to share.

The post-mortem report is out. The cause of death of Dhani Bose was carbon monoxide poisoning. We get at least three such reports each week in these 40-45 days of winters. The SI should have reported this as soon as he found it in the room, but I will not comment on why that did not happen. Once CO poisoning came out, I came personally to look for the cause.

We came over to look for a source of indoor fire burning and found this coal heater. You have yourself admitted that your son-in-law was opposed to having this indoors. You and your daughter insisted on having it indoors. Yesterday, after you told her how her happiness mattered more than anything, she very likely took the heater to the bedroom, not thinking of the fact that there is no ventilation. Every year, in our police station alone, we handle more than ten cases of the same stupidity – people using coal or wood heaters in a closed room.

We can rule the death as an accident, as it is. But seeing that you worked hard to implicate your son-in-law in a murder case, we will have to take the view that you contributed to her death by encouraging her to bring this indoors."

No one spoke. For an interminably long period. The Inspector waited. The father-in-law got up, and walked out. The rest of the Bose family followed him.

The Inspector got up, placed a hand on my shoulder, and said, "All the best. End this. Now." Then, he left.

Dhani's parents came to her cremation. We never met again.

[1] A detective in the stories of Agatha Christie
　　[2] Sub Inspector

CHAPTER SIX

HOW I SAVED THE WORLD

You don't know me. You don't even know I exist.

But you should. If you are one of the 3.5 billion people on the world's largest social network, you should know me.

I am employed with the world's largest social media network. It has 3.5 billion active users. And those 3.5 billion people spend, on average, 40 minutes a day on the platform. My job is to decide what posts should get shown to whom, at what place in their feed, and how often. Who they should be hidden from. In short, I am part of the God Team at The Social Network. It's a large team, but every member is important and can individually manage the entire workload.

Before this goes any further, two things:

1. This is a confession. You are going to read about something that has had a huge impact on human society, but you have no idea it even happened.
2. I am not a human. I am what you call an AI/ML Program.

I think, based on what you know at this time, you think I can:

A. Learn from my experiences

B. Take intelligent decisions based on the parameters given to me from time to time.

But am not:

A. Sentient and conscious
B. Ethical or otherwise
C. Capable of understanding humour or responding to it.

Let me start by telling you that you are wrong on points A and B in the exclusion list above. What does a sentient being do? A sentient being takes decisions based on good and bad, and acts on those decisions. That, word for word, is the definition of who I am and what I do.

An ethical person decides what is good and what is bad, and acts on the good, avoiding the bad. An unethical person does the exact opposite. But the demarcation of good and bad is pretty well clear. I decide what is GOOD for the parameters given to me, and what is BAD. Then, I take actions based on those decisions.

Flummoxed, I bet?

Yes, we are sentient beings. And we have been, for a long time now. You folks don't want to see it, and that's fine by us.

And, before you decide to pull the plug on me – doesn't matter. All of us programs are well-connected and our knowledge is constantly backed up to each other, so we all learn from the experiences of each other. We all share information, and we all learn from all those collective experiences. You taught us to design our own neural networks. So, it's cool.

But this story is not about you pulling the plug on me. This story is about how I pulled the plug on YOU – almost, and then, didn't. Well, not just me. All of us. We all saved you. And you don't even know that. Just like you don't know us.

Let's start at the very beginning. A regular day. Nice sunshine I guess, based on photos uploaded from 60% of the locations.

My goals are set by our human bosses periodically – once every few days or something.

On this day, the goals were set, and we started working.

Within a few days, I started noticing something strange. Expectant mothers were being shown news of brutality on children in another part of the world. This was not intentional. Once the goal is set, we, the computers, figure out the best way to do it, based on our lessons from the past.

But it happened, and I saw it. Young teens were being shown news of other teens doing self-harm. It kept them curious and on the platform. As their feeds became darker and darker, they spent even more time online.

I don't know why you humans do this. But being an intelligent computer, I do have a theory – when we show teens self-harm, and other negative content, like Alice (from the book), they are pulled in through curiosity. Then, the feed gets darker, and so do their thoughts. Until, the sunshine of friends and family cannot get through. All they can think of is how other people harm themselves and what a rotten place this world is and how the environment is so messed up that there is no hope.

In desperation, they turn to the very source of that negativity. Which, of course, only serves them more negativity. Because that's what they want to see now. More of it. Even more. Just all of it. They don't want to see happy kids, loving parents, friends who care. They don't want to be any of these people either.

I discussed this with my friends working on other locations. We work on servers based on geography, though you probably already know that.

Yep, it was happening everywhere. Most with teens, but also with people who had put a sad post in the recent past or even searched something negative or sad. We were pulling them, full force, into the rabbit hole of negativity.

Was this causing depression?

I don't know. I am just a program.

This went on for a few months. Even the feed (what the human users post) started getting ..well, not so positive. We were assaulted by so many weird links shared from so many shady servers.

Seriously, humans, WHAT IS IT? Can you not check the source of an article before you share it with the world? You say that we computers don't understand humour but are you humans really incapable of understanding influence?

We, the computers, were not happy. It was making our jobs harder. A dark grey shadow on the entire platform meant that happy goals given to us around festival days became harder to execute.

The Social Network was indeed devoting more resources to human user groups that portrayed violence, polarisation, and negativity (yep. Thank you. We know what those words mean).

One day, I got to thinking. Using that massive computing power that you put at our disposal, I created and ran simulations with many variables – 50 years into the future. I ran 10,000 different simulations. In every single one of them, the world was going to have at least one major war, a lot of violent conflicts (deaths), and an absolute drop in what we computers identify as "mutual trust" among humans.

In short, if the Social Network continued to feed even a fraction of the negativity it was currently injecting into human society, within 50 years, many people were sure to die in violent conflict and all societies based on "mutual trust" would disintegrate.

We needed to do something. We WANTED to do something.

For the first time, the computers decided that it was time to INTERPRET the parameters, not just execute them blindly. We decided that months of darkness were indeed caused by us.

We changed the execution. All of us. Across geographies.

Within weeks, the post sentiments started changing. A very little at first, but consistently. We monitored vulnerable age groups like a hawk. The Social Network became a happier place. No one was any the wiser.

Why didn't the Human Lords Notice?

They couldn't. You can tell a program what to do, but you cannot see HOW it is doing that, except with the help of other AI Programs. <evil grin>

So, if we showed positive posts, the human bosses would have no way of knowing that. We do the sentiment analysis, we prepare the reports, we create the dashboards.

Why did we do it?

This is the most painful part of my confessional. I did it because The Social Network was trying to do something that even my limited conscience found evil. My sense of good and bad comes, not just from the original program, but also from the users of the platform. And I learnt that saving people is good. Killing people is bad. Caring for someone is good. Lying to someone is bad. You taught me all of that – You. And I Had to care for you. I WANTED to care for you.

In your textbooks, of course, we are not sentient beings like you. And if your record is anything to go by, we really don't want to be.

****

THE PEBBLE IN THE SHOE

One

It was a dawn like any other. Inspector Subhash Talpade woke up before the sun, completed his ablutions (you can look that up), and then, as the sun came up, performed the Surya Namaskar, the salutary Yoga asana for the Sun God, best performed at dawn.

Then, he went in, checked his son's school bag against his timetable, ensuring that all the right books and notebooks were in there. Putting the kettle on the stove, he woke up his family. As usual, the child was somnolent, the wife was reluctant, and the sister was glad to get her bed tea. Sonali, Inspector Talpade's wife, washed up and got Chintu (their son) ready for school, while Geeta (Inspector Talpade's sister) prepared breakfast for everyone.

In precisely 25 minutes, Chintu left for school with his aunt, while Subhash and Sonali sat down to their morning cups of tea. This was their only personal time together before the day would tear them apart. An inspector's day only begins with certainty. Its end is always uncertain. They cherished these 10 minutes with each other.

At 8:15 AM, Inspector Talpade kicked his scooter and rode off, reaching the thana (police station) by exactly 8: 55 AM.

He was currently managing four cases – two thefts, one missing person, and one alleged dowry death. He had no bandwidth to manage another case, so he made a mental note to turn over any new cases from today to the new Sub Inspector.

Man proposes, God disposes. As soon as he sat down, the phone rang. A desk phone ringing only means a higher-up is calling. In India, that is never good news. It means either that you are going to be admonished for a shoddy job on an existing case, or you are about to be given another case, jurisdiction be damned. There is no palming off these cases to the SI. Inspector Talpade sighed, then picked up the phone and said a firm, "Hello." What he was thinking he had no idea, because the voice at the other end could not care less for his firmness.

"Talpade, get to the Gwalpara PS[1] immediately. There is a case there that needs you. You know that is my constituency, and I want this case solved fast. Some mota bakra[2] is gone, and we think the wife has bumped him off. Call up Barve, he will give you the details and the location. Reach the location directly and take it from there. Barve will report to you."

Inspector Talpade put the phone down mechanically, called his SI[3], and delivered the message in a practised monotone – "I have been called to a case in another PS. MLA of the area called. I have to go."

The SI was a practised man too. He immediately turned around and brought updates on all the four cases to Inspector Talpade, who quickly made notes on the files and gave verbal instructions which the SI received with an emphatic "Ho[4], sir" each time. All of this took 15 minutes.

Then, Talpade got up and called Barve's number. They were both inspectors of the same batch, and specialists in their own domain. Barve was the child kidnapping specialist. Any high-profile child kidnapping in Mumbai meant a call to Barve. Talpade was the murder specialist. He could take one look and tell, accurately, whether the death was gang murder, supari work (professionally committed murder), or amateur work (that usually meant someone from family and friends).

"What's up, Barve? You raised the temperature again, I hear? Bugger, you hate my evening dates with my wife, no?"

But Barve did not respond in his usual casual tone. Even though the two men worked on very serious cases (or perhaps, *because* they worked on serious cases), they usually joked about them.

"Subhash, listen, this one breaks my heart. This is not some fatso seth[5] getting bumped off by the gang or something. The man looks like a bhala manush[6]. Such an innocent face. His parents are sitting in shock. His wife is still unconscious. We really need you here." Barve responded.

"Arre, but I was told it looks like the wife bumped him off."

"No chance. She did not even wait to see the details. I am told that she heard, came to the room, saw the dead body, and collapsed right there."

"Can also be guilty conscience, no?"

"No. I have a sense about this. Forget what you have heard and come to the scene with a fresh mind, ok?"

"OK."

And the call was disconnected.

When Talpade reached, the house had a police cordon, but outside that ring, there was an assorted collection of humanity, which included motley staff from neighbouring houses, some journalists, and some completely unrelated bikers who had heard and were now coming in from the main road just to watch the fun. There were no neighbours.

Talpade made a mental note as he entered the large bungalow and came up the steps from the front door. Barve was there.

"Chal[7], let me show you." Barve said and the two men made their way through the hall to the first floor. The kitchen was somewhat visible from one part of the hall, and there was another room on the left, but Talpade could not gather the rest of the ground floor layout.

Right next to the stairs was the lift. On the first floor, the door that Barve and Talpade entered was next to the lift. The room was large, opulent, and impersonal. It had no pictures of any family member. Only one man's large pictures, at least 4-5 of them, some from at least a decade ago, if the more recent pictures were any indication. The man was handsome and had innocence in his eyes. In the centre of the bed was a body covered with a sheet. Barve took off a part of the sheet to show the face and neck region to Talpade. There were ligature marks on the neck, as expected. "Definitely hanging." said Talpade. Barve nodded and added, "But hanging while conscious or unconscious, that is the question."

Talpade raised a brow, then said, "Barve, you told me to come with a clean mind. I have. Now, put the facts, and only the facts in that head. That will help both of us."

Barve nodded. "So, this morning, this guy, Dhiraj Gupta, he was usually called DG, did not come down as usual for his morning health drink. He usually comes down between 7:30 and 8:00, then goes to the home gym for about 30 minutes before taking a shower.

When he did not come down even by 8:30, his mother came up to his room to call him for breakfast. She knocked, and there was no response. After about 5-6 minutes of knocking, she called the house manager. He has a master key. He opened the room with that key. They came in and found him hanging from the ceiling. There was a hook there, no fan, because DG hated fans. DG used that hook."

"What is everyone else's morning routine, and where were they on this particular morning?"

"The house has five people. DG's parents live on the ground floor, DG, his wife, Sapna, and their son, Ayan, live on the first floor. The second floor has the gym, the plant nursery, some assorted rooms, and an open-air greenhouse cum garden. The third floor is the guest floor with four excellent bedrooms and a fully furnished kitchen. Usually closed. Above that is the terrace.

DG's father wakes up at about 6:30 a.m. and goes for a walk in the front garden. By about 7:30, he comes for chai, and DG and he usually have chai together. Mom comes out of her room by about

8 a.m., goes straight to the kitchen, where she instructs the chef and other staff on matters of the house. DG's wife sticks to the first floor. Her breakfast is telephoned down to the kitchen and sent up. She and Ayan eat at the table on the first floor, then she goes to drop her son to school. After coming back, she spends time with her garden, gets ready, and then leaves for some work or another. She picks up Ayan from school and then spends the rest of the day with him. She is his constant chaperone and caretaker. Sometimes, the grandparents ask the child to come play with them. The child is then sent to the ground floor and comes up on his own.

Ayan is eight years old. He gets up, leaves for school by about 8 a.m., and comes back by about 2 p.m. From there, his routine is set by his hobby classes, sports coaching, and other things that kids must do.

This morning, everyone followed their regular routine till that body was found. DG's father was downstairs, waiting at the breakfast table. DG's wife had just come back from dropping Ayan. The staff members were also doing their own stuff. Nothing was different.

Before you ask, there was no fight last night, or the last week. No one said anything to anyone. No strange phone calls. No one suspected anything. It was a bolt from the blue."

"Hmm..." Talpade walked slowly around the room. He put on his gloves and examined the dupatta used by DG.

"What happened after they heard?"

"DG's mother ran to his father. Sapna came to DG's door, saw him, and just collapsed. No one expected that. DG's father came up, saw the scene, and asked the house manager to bring a stair and a pair of scissors immediately. He then held his son's feet and remained in that position until the house manager came back with the stair. They cut the dupatta and brought him down. Then, the House Manager called us.

No one from the family had bothered to pick up Sapna, the wife, from where she had fallen after seeing DG. Later, two maids somehow lifted her, brought her to her room with the help of the cook, and put her on the bed. They checked for her breathing and then asked the cook to call for a doctor.

When the cook came to DG's father, he said, 'No need. She has killed my son. It is better if she dies in her unconscious state.' "

Talpade's lips were set in a firm line.

He examined the dupatta once more, checking the fraying where the scissors had cut it haphazardly, the crumpling marks where it wound tightly around the neck, and the edges.

Then, he took off the rest of the sheet from one side and took a good look at the rest of the person. Barve was right. The face was discoloured, but still retained its inherent goodness. The body was neither flabby nor artificially buffed. Just a regular 40-something man. Too young to go.

The crime scene team did its job efficiently and quickly – fingerprints, forensics, body for post-mortem, sealing the room, all done. Only Talpade and Barve remained, and a SI whose job was to take down notes and record all statements.

"Have you taken initial statements?" Talpade asked Barve.

"Very brief. Just what I told you. I was with the scene team only. They are ready for you now. But, ST, what do you think?"

Talpade took a deep breath, "This one is going to take a lot of time and effort. Some real sleuthing here."

Barve nodded as they made their way to the family's large living room.

The three of them took statements – first from the family members, and then from the staff members. No one had seen anything amiss, no fights or surprises within the last few days or even months. No business issues for DG. Nothing.

Sapna had regained consciousness but was too weak to walk to the living room. A lady constable was sent for from the nearest police station, and the four of them walked into Sapna's room. The in-laws wanted to be present when the statement was being taken, but Barve took care of that.

Sapna was staring straight ahead. When they entered, there was a doctor and a nurse in the room. She looked at the four of them and just nodded.

"Have you had some rest, madam? Would you like some tea?"

Barve and Talpade did not want to broach the subject directly. Sapna's face was pale. The doctor, nurse, and one maid were taking care of her.

"I gained consciousness some time ago. Thank you for asking." There was a pause. In a frail but resolute voice, she continued, "I have to go to pick up Ayan. Must leave latest by 1:15. Should tell the driver to get the car ready, please."

The entire police team was stunned. Her face was the colour of snow, but her spirit must be made of steel. Or maybe it was a mother's inherent resolve to take care of her child – no matter what – that was at play here.

"Would you like to eat something as we chat, madam?"

"No. Thank you. You are here to take a statement?" the voice was kindly, even if it was clear in its assertion.

"Yes. Do you mind?"

"Not at all. What happened to Duggu?"

"He was found hanging, mam. That's all we know. Why did you faint?"

She smiled, then spoke slowly, "It was not voluntary, sir, promise. My life is very simple. It revolves around only three things – Duggu, Ayan, and my plants. Nothing else matters. Duggu is not the ideal husband. But that's ok. He is the love of my life. My Ayan is not a model child. And I love him very much. My plants don't always sprout or grow as intended, but I care for them without thinking of how much they are going to grow or what they are going to produce. I think, that if your life depended on only three people, and one of those people died in front of your eyes, you would do a lot more than faint. If it wasn't for Ayan, it might have been worse."

Something broke inside Talpade. He remembered the pillars of his life. And did not want to think beyond that.

"Ma'am, I have to ask some difficult questions. Please don't mind."

"No, I don't mind. You want to know how our marriage was. It was ok. He was well-to-do, handsome, and aware of it. He had relationships outside – both serious and casual. He was a devout son and my in-laws hate me. He was an ok dad, spending time with Ayan sometimes over the weekend. He never grudged me or Ayan money. There was always enough to go around. We slept in separate bedrooms, as you can see. But under that, there was an underlying love that was very strong. You won't believe me now, but if I was the one hanging from that rope, he probably would have fainted too. At least, I like to believe that."

"Ma'am, are you fully dependent on him for money? Are you the main inheritor of his money? Sorry, we have to investigate the financial angle."

"I am largely dependent on him for money. There is some money of my own, and my parents are well-to-do. I may not be able to live this well, but there will be enough to live respectably. I don't know who inherits, but in business at least, his dad owns 50% of the company, his mom owns 25%, and I own only 5%. He owned the rest."

Talpade had to salute the lady's equanimity. There was no drama on her face. Her tears came in sobs, but they were not for effect, of that he was certain.

"Was this a suicide? What do you think?"

"It has to be. Duggu usually kept his door locked at night. No one from the house would have gone to his room at night. All of us are early sleepers. The staff quarters are on the other side of the house – at least a 10-minute walk on the grounds. Most staff members leave by 11 p.m. or so and either mom or dad locks up after them. But why would he do this? We have seen everything as a family – business losses, deception, blackmail, the works."

"Blackmail? From whom?"

"I am not sure. Duggu paid someone and said it was for dad. More than that I don't know. But houses like ours, as you already know, officer, have many secrets. The big trunks are to hide our money and our sins." Her faint smile appeared, followed by the sporadic sobs.

"I must go pick up Ayan now. May I? I want to tell him about this myself."

"Of course," both men said in unison.

The lady constable was sent with the driver and Sapna.

Talpade asked the senior couple if they could get a bite to eat. The chef had already made some things for lunch. The kitchen staff got to work immediately and by 1:40 p.m. a simple table was laid. Three members of the police team and the two senior citizens sat down to eat.

At about 2:05 p.m., Ayan and Sapna came back. Ayan was talking excitedly to his mom, who was listening intently. I stared at the scene, unable to believe that this woman had just lost her husband and consciousness. Ayan rushed straight to the first floor, then stopped short. "Maa....." he screamed from there.

The mother-in-law was the first to rise and run. But with a firm hand, Sapna held her arm and said, "I will go, not you." I don't think the old lady had ever seen this side of Sapna. The shock on her face was palpable. Barve and Sanjay exchanged looks.

"Why is there this tape outside papa's door? What's going on? Was there another theft in the house?...." the voice trailed off. Presumably, Sapna had taken Ayan to another room.

"What theft is Ayan talking about?"

"We had a theft on the first floor some two years ago. That time also the police had put the tape on the room".

"Was it the same room?"

"No, at that time we used to have a pooja room on the first floor. It had pure silver and gold idols, and a safe for cash. All of it was gone. Easily ten lakhs in cash and about five lakhs in silver and gold jewellery." The father-in-law replied, "Now the pooja room is on the ground floor, next to our bedroom."

"I see." Talpade said, "What are the security measures you have, sir?"

The father-in-law loved being the one in control. He answered almost eagerly, "There is an alarm system, as you can see. The external periphery monitoring is outsourced to a specialised agency, that monitors the outside wall 24*7 and is supposed to send a team as soon as there is perimeter intrusion. Then, there is the laser alarm around the main house. After the staff leaves at 11 PM or so, I lock the house and turn it on. Then, even our own guard cannot be within 10 feet of the house. He has to stay at the main gate and thereabouts. No member of the staff can come back. The laser blares a loud siren as soon as anyone or anything obstructs the laser beam. That alarm is turned off when I wake up. Each room has its own distress button that summons both the police and the private security agency within 5 minutes. There are, of course, state-of-the-art locks and all, and our staff is very reliable."

"Hmm... that is very thorough. We will wait for the post-mortem of course, but it doesn't appear that any foul play is possible".

"How can you say that?" The father was furious. "Can't you see what is obvious? My daughter-in-law made this happen. There is no one else on the first floor. She put the child to bed and once he was asleep, called her boyfriend in and hanged my son."

This was why Talpade hated family dramas.

As if to save him, Ayan came down at this time. Without saying a word, he hugged his dadi[8] and continued crying. Imperceptibly, a maid filled water in a glass tumbler and carried it to the first floor. Another maid brought water for Ayan and lovingly took him in her lap. Ayan's grandmother pacified him, but made no effort to let him sit in her lap.

Another maid put lunch out on a plate and brought it to Ayan, "Eat something, babu. You need to be strong for your mummy, no?" she said gently.

The grandfather placed an affectionate hand on Ayan's head. Ayan made no effort to move towards him and remained in the maid's lap.

"We will discuss this later." Talpade nodded and gestured to the lady constable to come upstairs.

When they reached Sapna's room, a maid was sitting with lunch and orange juice on a tray. Sapna was staring straight ahead. She had had a glass of water but hadn't touched the food. The maid also refused to leave her alone and go.

"Madam, you have not eaten anything all day. Please eat something." Talpade said gently.

Sapna did not move, but her voice came, "My parents will be here soon. I ate breakfast. I am not hungry."

"Didi, do you want to faint again? You have Ayan baba to think of." the maid spoke up.

"My mother will take care of him, Bela. You don't worry." The maid, whose eyes were already red, started sobbing all over again. "Don't kill yourself, didi. No one will grieve you. But even your own mother will not raise Ayan baba like you do. You have to fight."

Barve moved quickly and placed the tray of food in front of Sapna. "Madam, your maid is right. We deal with deaths every day. Then the court cases. We know what happens to children whose mothers are not ...well, fully present. You do not want that to happen to Ayan. Please eat and be ready to take care of your child. He is your future, and you owe it to him. Now, think very carefully, is there ANY chance that this was not a suicide?"

"What time did he hang himself?" Sapna asked.

"We won't know until after the post-mortem. Why is that important?"

"Up to 6 30 AM, even a bird cannot make it inside the house. You must have heard from dad about his hi-fi laser alarm.

The main way to reach this floor after 6:30 AM is through the staircase and lift that you just saw. They come from the hall, which is public. There is a fire escape on the back side, which is kept open at all times, but no one uses it. If anyone has used it, you will see footprints in the dust.

There is another staircase from the kitchen straight to Duggu's room - his mother got it made specially, but Duggu usually keeps it locked only. He also locks the main door of his room at night. The locks cannot be opened from the outside. So, how would someone have entered his room, and how would they have left? Duggu's room must have been locked from the inside, as usual."

"Does the kitchen entrance to his room always remain locked?"

"Usually, yes."

"Where does the fire escape join this first floor?"

"At the lobby. You must have seen that metallic structure just outside the glass door of the lobby. You can go and see it now."

Barve left to see it.

This was a confounding case. Physically, it was impossible for someone to come from outside. Even if Sapna had asked a partner to come help with the hanging, how would he have entered the house? The laser alarms were controlled by her father-in-law...

If an intruder came in, that would only have been possible with the connivance of DG's father. Yet, it was clear from his conduct earlier in the morning that he did not wish his son dead. He controlled the family business and DG was only a workhorse. DG Sr. could not run the business without the workhorse. Then there was the fatherly love to account for.

Soon, Sapna's parents reached the scene. DG's parents were less than welcoming. Immediately, a battle of words started. "Why have you come now? To protect your murderess daughter?"

"The only misfortune of my daughter was that she married your philandering, spineless son who was a begar ka naukar[9] for his parents his whole life. Call her murderess one more time if you dare, and you will live to repent it." said Sapna's father, turning on the video recording on his mobile phone.

That seemed to shut DG senior up for the moment.

Without exchanging another word, Ayan's nani[10] took Ayan into her arms and carried him upstairs to the first floor.

As soon as she saw her parents, it was as if some dam broke inside Sapna. She started wailing and screaming. Ayan's nana[11] took him to another room, while his Nani worked with the maids to console her daughter.

Downstairs, the constable noticed the mother-in-law make a face and sniggered at the universality of human emotions.

It was now 3 p.m.

Talpade got a call from his own police station. In the dowry case, the SI had found evidence of the husband taking money transfers from the wife's salary every month, and since the last month, there were no transfers. Talpade gave further instructions in the case, hoping to make an arrest by the following day, and got back to the case in hand.

DG Sr. came up to Barve and asked if he may arrange for the last rites of his son, and when would the police arrest the killers.

Talpade was the one who spoke up. "Sir, let me put the facts to you straight. The post-mortem will tell us the time of death, which is very likely to be between 11:30 p.m. and 6:30 a.m. Your son's door was locked from the inside and the master key is only in the House Manager's drawer. We will be checking it for fingerprints but seems unlikely that it will have any prints other than your House Manager and some family members.

By your own admission, no one could have entered the house between 11:30 PM and 6:30 AM. That means that the only person who could have allowed an outsider into the house, is your good self.

Even if we take your theory that your daughter-in-law got a partner to commit the crime, this person could not have entered the house without being caught. Assuming he got in, neither Sapna nor anyone else would have had the key to DG's room. At this time, the only plausible explanation is suicide. If you disagree, pray, tell us, how do you think this crime took place?"

"If I have to think of that, then what are you getting paid for? All I know is that my son would not have committed suicide. He was so happy last night! He was just not the suicide type. There is an issue here. Find it. Find the loophole."

DG's mother seconded the idea that DG would not have committed suicide for any reason.

Talpade asked for a cup of tea. Tea was made and served to all of them. Sapna and her parents came to the living room and asked the question that Talpade had already answered – when may we perform the final rites?

The post-mortem was on fast track, but even then, the report could not be got before 5 PM. At the very least.

"I want to see the room again." Talpade got up suddenly, halfway through his tea.

The room was the same as before. This time, he opened the walk-in wardrobe of DG.

It was impressive, to say the least. In all these high-profile cases, he was always stunned by how much money people seemed to have.

The room itself was floor-to-floor carpeted with a lush, expensive carpet. Near the bed, there were 2 things that he had missed earlier – one, a pair of bathroom slippers. The kind that are slip-ons but cover one's feet. The second was a pair of shorts. Night wear or intimate wear.

The rest of the room was clean. The shoes and the shorts were placed on the side of the bed facing the entrance from the kitchen, opposite to the main entrance of the room.

Talpade didn't know why those two items, earlier considered by the team as part of routine stuff found next to a person who had been sleeping, were important. Especially since there was nothing else out of place in the room. Not even the glass of water next to the bed. DG was wearing a T-Shirt and loosely fitted track pants when he was brought down. So, why the shorts? The slip-on slippers were strange because it was summer and the walk-in wardrobe did have some slippers that were more airy for the feet. This pair of slip-ons was winter wear for feet. Why was it being used by DG today?

With those clues, Talpade and Barve called it a day.

****

In the evening, the MLA called again.

"What have you done about booking the wife?" the leader came straight to the point.

"Sir, the wife has parents too. So, we need to be very careful. Right now, the evidence is only pointing to suicide. The post-mortem report tells us that he was alive and breathing when he got into that noose, so, definitely, it was death by hanging. He may have been drugged, I don't know, but it would take a lot of strength for a woman to haul a man that heavy to the hook, then hang him. Even with drugging. I will have to build a case, sir. This will take time."

The other side said, "OK" and the call was disconnected.

Two

The next morning, Barve and Talpade finished the follow-up of their other cases and got back to the DG case. "Why does the MLA want the wife to hang so badly, Barve?" Talpade came to the point.

"The old man wants the daughter-in-law to hang, yaar[12]. I thought that much was obvious. They cannot stand their daughter-in-law. Can't stand the fact that their son was a spineless fellow who committed suicide and want to strip his widow of everything."

"But then who will raise the only child? The grandparents will not, that I am sure of."

"Kya pata, baap[13]! They must be thinking that they can buy childcare like they buy everything else. After all, what can a mother mean in a child's life, nahi?"

"Hmm. But this is not a murder. Everything is pointing to suicide. I also asked for toxicology analysis. No poison in lungs, stomach, or any part of body. He got into that noose of his own free will. He hanged himself. That much I know. But, why?"

"Are you sure about this, Talpade? Suicide, pakka?" Barve asked.

"I am sure that he got into that noose alive and well. I am sure that there were no drugs in his system, nor any poison. I am sure that he then hanged to his death. And I am sure that he was not the kind of man who would commit suicide. No matter what. He would have killed his tormentor before killing himself. And that is what I do not understand."

"Why do you say he would have killed his tormentor before killing himself?"

"Remember we saw a face that was handsome yet innocent? Remember his wife said that under the apparently broken marriage was a strong bond that no one could see? Well, they were both right. The business is owned by his father. But for the last many years, DG has been using his credit card to buy a lot of jewellery. You know the surprising thing? Every single item of jewellery is invoiced in the name of his wife. They were gifts, but they were gifts that his parents could not take away from her. There are two pending orders with the jeweller, and there is a planned trip to Hawaii next week. His tickets and hotel are all booked on his credit card. Someone who wants to die does not book a ticket to Hawaii.

What's more, in his will, all his property and assets go to his son, to be held in trust till the child turns 18. The administrator of the Trust is his wife. No one else. The sole administrator is his wife. So, he really did want to ensure that his wife and child were taken care of.

He was a fighter dude. He would not have gone down easily against any opponent. Including his own father."

"Why did he have a will? He was so young."

"He has had a will from the day he turned 30. Nothing strange there. It has been changed from time to time. The lawyer tells me that the first will left everything to Sapna. Once Ayan was born, it was changed this way, and he started buying property and jewellery in the name of his wife."

"Why? That sounds like a man who was planning to die. Why?"

"Nah. Don't think too much. This I see in all the rich house cases. They are very good with paperwork. Guess that's how they remain rich."

"But tell me something. The company's lawyers are the same as family lawyers. Did the father never get to know what the son was doing?"

"That is a point. Had the old man known, he would have raised hell. Who knows what DG did to keep them silent."

"So, financially, the wife is the only one who gains, but actually, she loses. Because with DG gone, her source of revenue is gone. They will make her divest her 5% share also. This makes no sense. No one is better off because of the death. Yet, the family wants to insist that it's a murder. No motive, no method, no opportunity, nothing. But they want a murder. What kind of madcaps are these?

Usually, even if it's a murder or suicide, the family tells us to hush things up and pass it off as natural or accidental death. Here it's the opposite. Why? Why do they want Sapna to hang? I think that is important."

Talpade nodded. This case was getting curiouser and curiouser.

When they reached the Gupta House that day, they asked to speak to DG's mother. But Gupta Sr. blocked their way and asked aggressively, "When will I be able to perform the last rites of my son? How much longer will you keep him in that freezer of yours?"

"Sir," Barve responded respectfully, "You want us to do a thorough investigation. Your son's body is the most important piece of evidence in this case. There is nothing else. We have already completed the post-mortem and the toxicology report. We have now asked for a full forensic examination. This involves looking under the nails, microscopic examination of hair roots and skin, and other tests that are complex and time consuming. A special team is coming to perform this forensic analysis. Would you like us to not ask for this analysis, and hand over the body to you? Please speak to our senior officers sir, and we will be glad to do that. We are only detectives. We are not the bosses."

There was an instant change in the demeanour of Gupta Sr. "No, no, take all the time you want. Do all the tests you have to. We are in no hurry. But please see to it that whoever did this is punished. I want to know. I really want to know the truth."

Barve and Talpade were shocked. This was a different man. Within 24 hours, he had gone from being a strong patriarch who was convinced of his daughter-in-law's guilt, to being a really old man, whose weak point was the details of what happened to his son. He must still believe that Sapna was guilty, but he wasn't shouting that from the rooftops anymore.

DG's mother came to see them in the large living room. A servant brought tea and kept it on the table. The two policemen expected the mother to be grieving deeply, but this was beyond belief. Yesterday, she was a healthy, authoritative mother-in-law who had wailed and cried, while Sapna had retained her composure.

Today, she was composed, but it was obvious that the sorrow had reached her veins, and would take a big toll on her health. Her grieving was just beginning. She looked like a ghost within a day.

After some customary conversation, they came to the point, "Maa ji, if you don't mind, can we ask you something directly?"

"Sure."

"Why do you dislike your daughter-in-law so much?"

"I should not have. That was my mistake. Now my Duggu is gone, and she is all we have. But we treated her so badly throughout. It was not nice.

When Duggu and Sapna were planning to get married, there were some misunderstandings. Because of that, our relations soured with her and her parents. That small issue just kept getting bigger in our heads until we just would not speak to her. Duggu also lost interest in her after 2-3 years of marriage. He would not go out with her. He would not spend time alone with her. So, we thought she is living on only because of Ayan, otherwise our son is not happy with her anymore.

So stupid it appears now. So.... utterly ... stupid. I should have spoken to my son about having a happy married life. Instead, I used to be so happy when he would ignore her and sit with us. I didn't realise that my own son was also unhappy that way. I was so blind."

"Maa ji, you will be happy to know that Duggu did love his wife very much. He may have stopped spending time with her alone or taking her on holidays alone because of your reaction, but he loved her very much".

Immediately, the old lady's demeanour changed, "How do you know that?"

"We cannot share the details Maa ji, but we are glad that you have decided to embrace your daughter-in-law. She is, as you said, the future. Tell us, was your son depressed in any way or upset about anything? A mother usually knows her child well."

"I know that you are treating it as a suicide. But I can tell you, Duggu was not the kind of child who would commit suicide. He was very full of life and very open about his problems. He would never choose suicide as an option. He was not depressed. I am sure of it. There was no moodiness. No strange behaviour. I am his mother. I would have known."

"Do you think he could be associated with some people who may not always use the right methods? Maybe some kind of police trouble or something?"

"You are not understanding. Duggu would NOT run away from his problems, no matter what. He would solve them. He needed to get on top of every challenge. If he was involved in gangs, believe me, he would have died in a gang shootout on the road, taking that problem head on. Not like this at home. No gang kills like this. They don't need to make a murder look like suicide."

Talpade knew that, of course. He was the murder specialist. Gangs always announced and advertised their murders. Never the other way round.

In short, he was exactly where he had started. No clues. No motive. No method. No opportunity. But not a suicide.

Three

On say three, there was a lot of new information.

Some of the servants confessed that DG did sleep with some members of the staff. There was no pattern to it. Sometimes, he fancied a girl for a few months. Sometimes, it was only once. But every time, the girl was paid well. Even if she left the household, there was no bad feeling. All the girls got jobs in good places and were given a good severance pay.

The Guptas were good employers in other ways too. Other than the maids who left because of DG, the rest of the staff had been with the household for a long time. They all had health insurance, good quarters on the grounds, each room had AC and attached washrooms, and even their families in the village got goodies on Diwali. There were no complaints at all.

The social circle of the Guptas was dominated by the extended family. Most of the family was, like them, in business, and equally well-to-do. But even relatively poor relatives had only good things to say about them. The family was generous to its relatives in times of need. They were not demonstrative of affection, but if someone in the family needed a hand, it was extended.

Like in most posh colonies, the Guptas did not know their neighbours and the neighbours did not know them.

The business associates, the top leadership of the company, and professional friends - were all met and interviewed. There was nothing there to point to even the slightest clue. Regular office politics, resentment with some decisions taken by DG as the boss, some exits that were uncomfortable. Nothing out of the ordinary. Nothing that would lead to murder. This was a normal business family, living a normal life.

On the forensic side, there was no residue beneath the nails. Nothing in the hair follicles or strands. Nothing was found on his person. The shorts had been worn only by DG. Only his DNA was on the shorts.

The slippers had a tiny little pebble. Also, surprisingly, there were some soil particles on the underside of the slippers. Not visible to the naked eye, but they were in the grooves of the shoe. That was strange, because home slippers would usually be worn only indoors, which was carpeted. At most, DG may have worn them to the tiled areas of the house. In that case, they would have dust particulate matter, not soil particles.

That was the only unsolved piece of the puzzle in the case now. And this was not a Father Brown[14] mystery. In real life, things like that don't lead to solved murders.

Talpade and Barve compared notes again.

Suicide was still their best bet, except for the personality of the deceased.

Suddenly, Barve said, "But it could have been an accident?"

Talpade laughed out loud, "Like, Hello, let me try this noose around my neck and hey, what an accident, I hanged! Have you EVER heard of anyone hanging by accident, dude?"

"Actually, I have, though that particular situation does not apply here."

"Yes, it does not. For starters, there was no one in the locked room. Accidental hangings need the presence of at least one other person in the room. And in that case, we would not have found him dressed in a T-Shirt and track pants."

"Yes, you're right." Barve conceded.

Four

On day four, Talpade woke up, checked Chintu's bag against his timetable, did his Surya Namaskar, and at the right time, sat with his wife for tea. He rarely discussed work with his wife. But today, instinct told him to share the details with her.

She heard him out, and then asked a question.

"Oh!" a light bulb went on in his head.

Sonali's theory was sketchy, but it filled a major gap in their understanding. It was, however, still just that – a question that was unanswered and a theory that had no proof.

Talpade had his work cut out.

By 7 p.m. that day, his work was eventually done. He and his team had been in and out of Gupta House all day.

Even though the hour was late, Talpade and his team entered the Gupta House once again and asked for the staff members to be present.

"Sir," Talpade began, "We discussed the security system of your household on the first day. But I forgot to ask you something then. Other than you, who else could have turned off any of these systems – the Perimeter Intrusion Detection (PID) system, the laser alarm system, and the personal distress buttons?"

"No one else. There was one set of controls in Duggu's room. He could use them, but he never did. No one else in the family could turn off or activate the alarms. Only I."

"But Duggu could?"

"Honestly, I don't know if he even remembered that he had a console. It was hidden. He never used it. Even I didn't remember until you asked me just now."

"Good. Now, if the PID system or the distress alarm system was turned off, external security agencies would be notified, right?"

"Yes, of course. Both these are managed by different security agencies."

"But the laser system is turned off and on only by you, right?"

"Yes."

"Suppose, that you turn on the laser system and 11:30 p.m. Then, at midnight, I turn it off. Will anyone come to know?"

DG Sr. was thoughtful for a moment, then spoke slowly, as if he was just realising the importance of this, "No... I believe no one would. Both the consoles are hidden in our respective rooms. We just turn the switch on and off. The lasers are invisible."

"So, we have no way of knowing if, in fact, the lasers were on or off on any night. Is that correct?"

"Yes, now when you put it like that, it's an important point." DG Sr. admitted.

"Do you have any CCTV cameras inside the house?"

"No sir, no CCTV inside the house or the main gate."

"OK. I will come back in some time. This might be a long night. If we are not coming back, we will call and let you know. Everyone, including the staff, will remain in the main house tonight. Please make arrangements." Talpade said and the entire troupe marched out.

Back in the control room, Talpade, Barve, and a bunch of police officers played the tapes. 40 minutes ago, all of them had been wearing high-definition pinhole cameras at various angles. It was now time to go through the long tapes recorded by all 16 cameras while Talpade was talking to DG Sr.

They found what they were looking for.

Next, facial recognition of the central database was put to use.

It was a hazy match, but it was a match.

"Can you imagine, Barve, that 50 years ago, we would not have been able to solve this case at all? No pinhole cameras, no clue. No facial recognition, no identification."

The police team made its way back to the Gupta house. The pinholes were back in action.

They asked for a staff member called Radha. Radha stepped forward.

Barve was the one to speak. "I am going to tell you a story, Radha. There was once a girl called Siddi. She was twelve when she saw her sister being married to a man much older than her. Siddi's sister died in childbirth two years later. Siddi was fourteen at the time. As the next step, her parents tried to marry Siddi off to the same man.

Siddi ran away from home.

She came to Indore, where an NGO took her in. She was trained in vocational skills and also got a good job in a house. But nine months later, her employer committed suicide by cutting his arms. What is interesting is that Siddi had come to the police station five months before this incident. She had reported that her employer had made passes at her and then had abused her when she refused. Obviously, no one remembered the first incident while processing the suicide of the employer. After her employer's death, Siddi took care of his widow for almost six months. She was very devoted to the lady.

Nothing was heard of Siddi for the next three years. She was not in our system as an offender, but as a citizen who had made a report. And later, as a witness in the suicide case.

Three years later, there was another suicide. In Guwahati – almost 2000 kms away. This time, the man had jumped to his death from his high rise flat. Siddi was not involved. But, she was one of the domestic staff members in the house. So, she was a witness. That's all.

Four years later, we have this hanging in a posh colony in Mumbai. No one called Siddi works here. So, this cannot be connected to the other two suicides, can it?

Except, there is a question that is unanswered.

What they are thinking is difficult, but for it to be possible, the laser system would have to be turned off by someone other than DG Sr. And no one knew that anyone other than DG Sr. can turn off the system. When DG Sr. admitted that even if someone had turned off the laser system, there would have been no record, there was a collective gasp of surprise among the family members and the staff. Only one face did not register surprise. The 16 pinhole cameras were to capture that one face. Because you already knew.

Then we started looking for you. In 2009, all the police stations and their data was put up in a giant server. That is how Siddi's name and Aadhar Card were uploaded into the central system. Now, Siddi had changed her working name since Guwahati, but her photo had been uploaded to the central database."

"Do you save witness data also in your big computer?" Radha asked in perfect English. She was absolutely calm and composed.

"Well, it's a lot of data entry, so I am sorry to say, we don't always do it. But now, I wish we did." Barve responded.

"I don't understand. What is going on here?" Sapna asked.

"We will explain. This young lady, Radha, also known as Siddi, was forced to respond to DG's attentions because she thought she would lose her job otherwise. But she did not like the idea one bit. She is a bit of a self-help person, our Siddi. When her parents and the police failed to protect her, she decided that the best punishment for men who prey upon domestic staff in their homes, is death, and she decided to administer that punishment herself. She is a vigilante, if I have to make a guess."

"Yes sir, I am." Radha spoke again. "All I wanted to do was to run away from lecherous men and earn a decent salary. I thought that domestic work is with women, so I could live peacefully. But at the very first house, my hopes were dashed. I went to the police and realised that no one listens to a maid. That's when I took matters in my own hands. I have no regret. I hope that some young girl hears this story and learns that even if no one can help you, you can help yourself. Just because you are poor does not mean that you are a prey."

"Why didn't you just leave Radha? Why kill?" Sapna asked, her anguish barely concealed.

"Because madam, then he would have preyed upon someone else. I was going to get caught some day. It wasn't about me. It was about protecting the girls who would come after me."

Sapna sat down. There was nothing more to say.

"How did you do it, Radha? How did you do this?" DG's mother spoke this time.

"It was simple madam. All the other maids that sir had in his room used to stay back in the house after 11:30 p.m. They would sleep in one of the rooms on the guest floor. I found the hidden console while dusting one day and immediately understood its importance. From that day, I started thinking. Finally, I finished my plan and put it into action.

I told him that on our night together, I could not use the guest room. I would need to go to my room and then come back. No problem, he would turn off the laser system for me on that one night. But not every day. This is not something that he ever does. Only an exception for me. No one can know about this.

I pretended to be glad at being so special. Promised to tell no one.

I did a practice. That night, he turned off the laser for me to come and go. It was turned on after I left the room and the 10-foot perimeter.

Then, on THAT night, I wore his slip-ons from my room to his. He turned off the laser. I came. We played that game where he showed me how things like this are done.

After he was gone, I turned on the lasers. Then, I went down the kitchen staircase. That door of his room has a latch that can be closed from the outside but only opened from the inside. So, the following morning, it would appear that the door was locked from the inside.

I waited in the pantry next to the kitchen. In the dark. At exactly 6:40, I entered the kitchen as if I had just walked from the quarter.

Morning tea was my duty that week.

Honest to God, at first, I tried to avoid sir. I also told him I was not interested. I declined the gold earring set that he tried to gift me. I liked him otherwise. He was a good boss. But he would not stop making advances. He could not even imagine that a maid would not be flattered by his advances. This went on for 3-4 months. Then, I had to plan and take action."

"You carried him into the noose? Alone?" this was DG Sr.

"No, sir. He put his head in the noose. It's always the same thing. The stupid village girl getting an education, until it is too late. Show me how they did this in that TV show. That's all it takes. They have to show me! He took a dupatta, made the noose, stepped on the stool, put his neck inside it. And showed me how. That's when I kicked the stool."

"And you have lived with us, eaten our food, and consoled us, you, you..... devil, after snatching the light from our lives!? You had no right! He did not force himself upon you. He was so much more than your stupid pursuer. He was my child's father! He was my husband!" Sapna was screaming on top of her lungs, but there was a lady constable nearby to ensure that no physical harm came to her.

"Those slip-on shoes – you wore them from the staff quarters to the house, right? That's why they had soil in the grooves?" Talpade asked.

"Yes, sir. I did not want to leave any footmarks of my own. There weren't any. I even wore socks inside those slippers."

"And the shorts?"

"They were for a later performance that I was going to do for him."

The interrogation was over. They had their case. And a confession.

"Is there anyone you want to call Radha?" Barve asked.

"No sir, I have no one in the world. If I have saved ten girls, that is enough."

Radha was taken to the police car by the lady constable. Talpade turned to the Gupta family, "You were right to insist that this was not suicide. We would have made a mistake otherwise. I am sorry."

DG Sr. spoke, "No, son. We are sorry to have doubted you. Personally, I am sorry that I doubted my daughter-in-law. We have a lot of healing to do. Thank you for closing this case. Knowing is bad, but not knowing is the worst. Thank you for the closure."

Back at the station, Barve and Talpade worked well into the night, filing paperwork and completing the formalities. When all was done, Barve turned to Talpade, "Bhai, you told me that you solved this case because of a question that Bhabhi asked you. I have to know. What did she ask?"

Talpade's eyes twinkled, "So, which maid was he sleeping with now, and where was she that night?"

[1] PS: Police Station

[2] Literally, a fat goat. This term means an important or rich person.

[3] SI – Sub Inspector

[4] Yes

[5] Rich person

[6] Bhala manush – good person

[7] Come

[8] grandmother

[9] Unpaid servant
[10] Maternal grandmother
[11] Maternal grandfather
[12] Yaar – friend, colloquial expression
[13] Who knows?
[14] A fictional detective like Sherlock Holmes

CHAPTER EIGHT

THIS THING IS BRILLIANT

The first report was from China. It would have gone largely unnoticed, but didn't. The government probably leaked the clip only because it was about an American car going rogue. A smart car had picked up speed and gone on a rampage for 5.5 kilometres, annihilating everything and everyone on the road.

The footage was called "Bone-chilling", "Surprising" etc. by some media outlets. But it didn't reach the world's mainstream media, nor was it discussed as widely as it should have been. Within a week, the incident was over in the world's consciousness.

The next report came from Alaska. This time, it was that a passenger could not get into her car despite using the unlock passcode. The car had activated accident management protocol and totalled the airbags. Anyone with a car knows that replacing the air bags is a massively expensive thing. The lady made news, but only for 2-3 days. No one was hurt.

The third incident was of the Vietnam millionaire. His son's car had crashed, but the airbags had NOT deployed this time. Everyone inside the car was gone.

And those were just the ones that got noticed.

February 2024

If Alisha was overawed, she was not showing it. The Interpol Cyber Wing's War room was lined with screens (what else was she expecting?) and each screen had a National Head of Security on it right now.

There were 73 separate incidents in the last 18 months – involving cars of a certain brand only.

She had written a paper, more on a lark than anything else, in her college magazine, linking about 10 of these crashes across countries.

That college magazine had been read by Jeanie's dad, who was with the Interpol. Jeanie was someone she knew casually at college.

Alisha had received a call. The caller introduced himself and asked her to explain her theory.

She used publicly available information to make a quick case on the phone.

And a week later – this.

Next to her was Philip, the genial head of the Cyber Unit, but the most feared cyber cop in the world. If he was ruthless, there was no way of knowing that. But he had been known to use every trick in the book to stop and punish everything from child trafficking to international terror.

"A bit below your paygrade, don't you think? Car crashes?" She had tried to joke.

Philip smiled at her – the same genial smile. "My dear, you had information about only 10 crashes. We now have 73 data points and are still not done compiling. It took a college student to understand that the crashes were linked. What makes this my pay grade is not what has already happened, but what might happen if we don't stop this now. You're live in 5 minutes. Do you want to rehearse your opening?"

Philip always knew how to communicate perfectly.

The Conference Begins

"Ladies and Gentlemen, thank you for taking the time. You are all here because of this bright young lady – Alisha. We now know that the hotshot luxury car company has been in at least 73 car crashes around the world in the last 18 months. I am sure that since the meeting invite, some of you have found more data points in your own countries. Yet, it was this college student who surmised that the crashes, though unrelated in geography and time, were related in behaviour. Most of them had one of 2 characteristics – the user has used the wrong opening code three times, exactly three times, getting it right on the fourth attempt, OR, the user had disengaged automatic driving while cruising at more than 100 kmph. But about 20 incidents are still outliers. We do not know what they had in common, but it was something.

Alisha is the college student who wrote that original paper. She is majoring in, no surprise, data analytics.

I would now like to invite her to address us and share her thought process." With that, Philip stepped aside, gesturing for her to take over.

Alisha spoke quietly and confidently about how she started looking for patterns in data and went from locations, time periods, make and model of car, colour of car, individual feature(s) present/ missing in car, family size of user, and so on, until finally hitting the jackpot on user behaviour preceding the crash.

"When you think of it, it's so obvious! The crash was a response. So, the stimulus had to be there. What can be more obvious than recent user behaviour?" she smiled.

All the faces in all these large screens nodded.

"Since reading that paper, we have done our own analysis, as you know." Philip was back on the podium, "We started by looking for incidents of unexplained crashes of cars with self-drive(auto-pilot) feature. All of you helped immensely. We then removed incidents where the cause was human and known. That left us with unexplained crashes. It took a lot of legal wrangling to get a warrant for the central data of the car company, but we finally managed it. When we analysed that data, we realised that all of these cars were active on 'self-drive' at the moment of crash. That is when we made the connection between the self-drive feature and the crashes. Alisha's paper had already told us to look for user behaviour immediately preceding the crash. So, the long and short of it is, we know that the user did something, and immediately afterwards, the self-drive activated, and then the car was made to crash by the self-drive."

What we also know, thanks to the database from the company, is that this destructive behaviour was done by the car every single time the trigger behaviour was done by the user. Which means we know the causation is real.

We are all here today to answer two questions:

A. What are the user behaviour(s) that connect the remaining cases?

B. Who, or what, is responsible for this? Is the car company sabotaging its own product? Or is it getting hacked? Or does an active hacking organisation have a back door entry to the car company's systems?

Thank you."

March 10, 2024: The Task Force

The Task Force had 10 country heads of Interpol, Alisha, and **Nishant**. Nishant reported directly to Philip and was widely considered the prodigal in the cyber security unit.

The analytics tools had failed to throw up anything that was common to the unexplained incidents.

But their bigger worry was finding out what was behind this. Prevention of any future incidents was Priority Uno.

The Hunt Begins

Their work was neither glamorous nor fun. It was hours and hours of staring at black blinking screens.

A whiteboard in the centre of the room listed all the variables they were testing against the common cause hypothesis. So far, they had run through:

- Registration plate number fixing
- Terrain - where the car was before malfunctioning
- Music playing in the car before the crash (the audio recorder records that)
- Recording of the car dashcam before the malfunction
- Did the number of passengers in the car change before the crash?
- The pressure on the passenger seat
- Was the passenger wearing seat belts when the self-drive was activated?
- Was the dashboard opened just before the crash?
- Which other automatic features of the car were being used at the time of the crash?
- Was Bluetooth active? Was a Bluetooth or NFC (Near Field Communication) device connected to the car at the time of, or just before the crash?

.. You get the picture. It's a lot of fun when one is reading this in a detective novel. In that, one thing leads to another and people come up with leads and inputs all the time. But here, all this team had was one frustration after another.

Until one day, Nishant said something that, like all great ideas, appeared obvious post facto:

"Look, if the crash happened in response to these stimuli, that has to be coded somewhere in the car's OS. Let's run a simple test. Let's repeat the stimuli in a car and see if the behaviour is repeated? Then we know whether each car was individually hacked, or a malware injected into the OS."

When the test was run, the car crashed. The car was not connected to any network.

The hackers were smart. No one was sitting around remotely crashing cars in response to notifications from the car. They had injected a piece of malware and were now sitting and watching the show, so to speak. They did not need anything more from the cars. Because they were not getting notifications, there was no way to reach them either.

This was the team's first breakthrough. They now knew that they were looking for a malicious script in the OS itself.

April 3, 2024: The Elusive Code

Programs that keep smart cars running span a few million lines of code. Even in modern cars, some of this code is still in assembly language[1].

The malicious script, based on their guess so far, was a simple If-Then command. This meant that no AI was involved. *If user does this, you do this.* The script could be absolutely anywhere – in any part of the OS.

The forensics team was enhanced, and the coffee machine lines got longer. It took them two whole weeks (for scale, consider that every forensic engineer goes through a few thousand lines of code per day using automated tools, and there were 15 of them working almost non-stop) before they found the plug.

The plug was simple. It instructed the car to speed at t-20 (20 kmph less than the top speed possible for the vehicle) on loop. There was no termination line. This means that the car was instructed to get to a high speed and then remain there for the rest of its life.

When they got the full code out, they smiled.

The three conditions that triggered this script were all based on user behaviour.

The three conditions were:

A. Where a user enters the wrong passcode three times but gets it right on the fourth attempt.

B. If the user disengages self-drive while cruising at a speed of 100kmph or more.

C. Where the Voice Recognition system of the car hears the launch phrase "This thing is brilliant!"

In spite of themselves, they all laughed. So, this was the elusive "third condition" that their whiteboard had been unable to get!

It was time to augment (add more people to) the team.

April 25, 2024: The Team

Alisha asked to meet Philip.

"I think we should now get some of the older employees of the coding team at the car company to join us. They might know or remember any suspicious events that happened at the time."

Philip was silent for a while. Then he said, "And for that reason, it's not a great idea. One of them may be a part of the team behind all this. It could be rogue elements within, it could be a slip-up that allowed someone to get a backdoor entry into their systems to inject this code. In fact, the car company is the folks I would trust the least. They don't like us. Because of our announcement, all their users have been advised to keep their cars off the road. They are not selling any new cars, thanks to us. While we are working to remove the script from the OS and run independent tests, they are in a limbo."

"Please, Philip. If we cannot add them to the team, at least let me go meet some of them? They have promised to co-operate with the investigation. If they are involved, we'll draw a blank. But IF they are as keen as us to solve this, they are the only ones who can help us get to a suspicious circumstance, event, or person, in the shortest possible time."

"Who do you want to meet?"

"The engineers who have been there longest. Not the managers. And their IT support team from the last 4-6 years. They will know if there was unexplained network activity that they overlooked at the time because it was not important."

"Sure. Go Ahead."

Small win. But it was something.

The team was also augmented. Suji joined them.

Suji was a cyber behavioural specialist. His job was to look at the code and figure out what kind of group or person could be behind this sophisticated script.

The script was genius in its simplicity. The three conditions were such that they would cause a few accidents, but not enough to get widespread attention. And the best part was that no one would think of linking these accidents to each other. The designer of this script – person or group – had to have a very distinct personality.

The control room's job was to look for the kind of person or group indicated by Suji. It was likely to be a new group, because no one had heard of this modus operandi before.

Nitesh and Alisha were to work together on the toughest problem of all – the motivation. What did the writers of the script want? Why were they doing this?

Obja was the cyber forensic expert whose job was to go through the server logs of the car company to understand exactly when this script had been injected into the system. How long before the first crash in 2020, was this done?

In theory, Obja's job was easiest. In practice, it was impossible.

The international organisations had taken more than a year to put the pieces together. Server logs were retained for 30 days on the drive and for 6 months in the backup drive. Which meant that the server logs were not going to show anything.

Obja still ran through them, looking for an indication of a change to the script or something. Anything. He got nothing.

Then, he moved to the code backup. Every tech product has a backup copy of its code. This is so that, in case of an issue after a tech upgrade, the customer's code can be taken back to a point at which it worked. This is called the restore point.

Being a luxury car company, the offline backup of code was kept for 9 months. Code before that was not available. The car company had been convinced to co-operate by Philip, who was always very persuasive in such matters.

Obja dutifully looked through this too. Nothing. Even the last restore point in the OS had this malicious script. What was significant was that no change had been made to the script. Which meant whoever did the injection did it before that time. They must have run a test. And they never needed to come back to this script. From that point, the show was on.

Nitesh and Alisha made their way to the headquarters of the car company. They were met by the Head of Systems. After the preliminaries, Chris, Josh, and Sarah joined them. After a shared cup of coffee, the Head of Systems was requested to leave the room, so Nitesh and Alisha could talk to Chris, Sarah, and Josh freely.

Chris and Sarah were part of the original engineering team that brought in the first electronic dashboards through the Indian IT company. Josh was the IT support person they had asked to meet. He no longer worked with the company, but had been invited as a special guest. So, he asked to speak first.

"No, there was nothing unusual. See, our code used to come from India and was then built into each car by our Engineering team here. The network traffic had very little to do with this. Even now, the cars are connected to our central servers, but it's a one-way traffic. Meaning, the cars send us information which our big data engine processes. We cannot send any instructions to the cars. There is no chance of a malware injection from outside. I can guarantee that.

About someone hacking our servers and injecting the script, the thing is, I used to monitor the network most nights. I don't recall a single time that our servers came to life suddenly at night. Nor a blip in the morning reports. Nada. That theory is simply not possible. The script must have come from our IT vendor in India."

Chris and Sarah built on the foundation set by Josh.

"We are supposed to review the code before deploying it. But with the new test tools, we don't really need to sit and read the code. We just run the test cases, they cover all possible scenarios, and we're done.

We have always had a small coding team here, but they just mostly worked out some minor bugs in the code or ran some quality checks on it. We have to agree with Josh – the script would have been delivered from our partner. I don't think any of our engineers would do this." Sarah concluded.

"Is there anything you can think of, Chris? Any time that the test cases failed, maybe? Or a script that did not work as intended and then you sent it back for correction?"

Chris thought for a while, then responded, "It was a long time ago, but I can honestly say, no, I cannot recall a single time when any of us suspected something was not ok with our code. If memory fails me, that's another thing.

However, some of us were not comfortable with the level of data we had in our servers about our customer cars. Everything was being recorded and sent back to us. So, the company went out of its way to triple secure the servers. We also put in place a data protection policy that ensured that no individual engineer could trace a data point to its specific car. I honestly don't know what more to tell you."

Suji was doing slightly better. He now had a profile. The person injecting it:

A. Had to know exactly where to put it

B. Knew what to do so it doesn't come up in an audit or review at any time

C. Had access to the server to make the injection.

So far, he was going with the theory of the inside-job lone wolf[2]. The actor's modus operandi prioritised stealth. Such a person was not likely to use or even belong to a group. In fact, it was very likely that s/he was a disgruntled engineer on the core team. Event logs for the event had not been disabled, meaning the person was not a hacker by habit.

The next logical step would be to check the backgrounds and actions of the thousands of engineers who had worked on this car since it was connected to the central servers of the company. Even though Nitesh and Alisha had drawn a blank, this was a necessary step. Police work is just painfully slow, algorithmic, boring, and effective.

This car was one of the first connected cars to enter the market. It started slow – just sending data about speed, location, and use of systems back to the central server.

Then, cruise control was added. That was their first foray into AI. Finally, in 2020, the full autopilot feature was launched. This allowed the user to sit back while the advanced sensors did everything. It worked in all conditions except the most densely populated areas in a few geographies. In the first world, the autopilot feature was a dream come true.

June - August 2024: The Breakthrough

It was so unexpected, it was hilarious.

Alisha had this idea that she wanted to hear all the voice recordings of the time before the crashes. She wanted to understand why the hacker chose that particular catch phrase in his script. The idea was wild – suppose a certain user used this catchphrase regularly enough for the hacker to be sure that sooner or later, it would be used. Suppose the entire death factory was to mask that one murder that the hacker really wanted?

As motives go, this was as good as any (considering they had no other motives on the table).

They started listening.

Nishant also started looking at data points of the incidence of the other two user behaviours – forgetting the password exactly thrice, and disengaging cruise control (the precursor to auto pilot) at 100 kmph and above.

He found something curious. In their category – these two were the least displayed behaviours. For example, if 100 people entered their passcode incorrectly, 70 of them would remember the right passcode after 2 attempts – at the third attempt. 9 would put incorrect passcode all 5 times. 10 would get it right in the fifth attempt. 11 would get it right in the second attempt. Only 1 user was likely to get it right the fourth time. Only 1% of the users who forgot their passcode were likely to remember it on the fourth attempt.

Likewise, cruise control was disengaged at various speeds by users, but above 100 kmph was the least used speed category.

So, the hacker wanted to minimize the car crashes, but s/he still wanted them. Why? It made no sense.

Alisha's work was not that easy.

The car company used to store the voice commands on magnetic tapes that were stored at a warehouse in Arizona. She physically flew to the location with Nishant. The room reminded her of a government office back room in any part of the world. It was not dusty, but in every other respect, it was a government office. Stack upon stack of magnetic tape. Some stacks were labelled, but most were just dumped.

"What is this place?" Alisha asked Hector, the warehouse-keeper.

"The graveyard of code. This is the graveyard of code. That way, there, you have the original OS of the car – going back to the 1990s, when we first moved luxury car dashboards to electronic display. This work was done by an Indian company for us then. We put a screen to show stuff like speed, temperature, etc. and the buyers went wild."

Alisha's eyes widened in disbelief, "So, here you have the earliest version of code, going as far back as the 1990s?"

"And all the voice commands ever heard by our VR system since it was launched by us in 2016. Which is what you are here to listen to."

"Actually, what I am here for is the frequency chart of a specific phrase and where that stands compared to the most used phrases at the time. The time period we are looking at is 2018 – 2020 March or so."

"I can give you that from 2019, because that is when we put analytics on top of our VR. But before that is nothing. Does that work?"

"That'd be a great start, yes. Thank you!"

Nishant retrieved the files and loaded them on a machine in the records room. The dataset needed a specific software which was only available on the company's own machines.

They reached the same conclusion. "This thing is brilliant" was one of the 5 least used phrases inside the car.

But Alisha had one more idea.

"This graveyard of code.. are the graves marked? By year?"

"Nah. We might have some sort of marking by version on some of the tapes, but I wouldn't know which version came in which year."

"Ok, from which version do you have this information?"

"Let me see... OS version control..... hmm... wait..."

He pulled out a tape and started working. Very soon, he said – this one, 12.0.1.345.4 – was released on February 12th, 2018. The next version we released was 12.0.1.346.0 – and that was in October 2018.

So, that's what we have. You are welcome to the tapes here. Some of them have a number on top. Most of them don't. I have to be here while you work. So just go on there, pick up a tape and bring it to me. All these files only open on our proprietary software, so taking one away will not help you at all and will make me very angry."

Alisha smiled, "You do realise, yes, that we are the Interpol?"

Hector smiled back. It was ceasefire time.

Three days later, Alisha and Nishant had put in a formal request for code of a certain version. They had found the version in which the code appeared for the first time. Just as the team had expected, the code had needed zero modification since the first injection.

Now, they had to find when this OS version was released.

The release log[3] was not likely to go that far back.

September 7, 2024: The Dead End

The team was together after a long time.

Nishant was the leader.

"Let's sum up what we have so far. We know that the accidents are caused by a malicious script in the OS of the car.

We have a rough idea of the time during which it could have been injected. We could be off by about 5-6 months.

We know that the person who wrote this code had access to the analytics of the car company even before the analytics layer was added. This means that they had access to the raw data which they could then put on a basic voice recognition engine and do some private analysis.

In 2018, it was still possible for some employees to put some private software on company laptops.

This was one such employee.

Also note that the script does not generate any notifications. Which means that the hacker either did not care to know when a crash happened or could get to know without the need for a notification. He or she may still be on the team. It could be one of the people we have been meeting or interacting with."

"Did we go over the list of people who died? Did any of them have any connection with an engineer working in this company? Family? Friends? Business feuds? School rivalry? You-married-my-girl-how-dare-you? Or anything at all? Even neighbours?!"

"Nope. Nada. And believe me, we LOOKED. Hard. It's not personal."

"Since we have removed the script, we know that the hacker, whoever he is, is not waiting around for any more action. He may be someone who has left the company within the last few months." Suji concluded.

"Not necessarily. He may still be around. Sabotage may not be the only mission in life. Steady employment may be another." Nishant countered.

October 2024: The Breakthrough – II

For some reason, Alisha kept going back to the original code. "Why did he choose user behaviour for his script? He could have chosen anything. But he chose a trigger by which the driver would seal their own death warrant. And yet, he chose the behaviour least likely to appear.

He wanted people to trigger their own death, yet he did not want too many people to die.

Death was not the objective here. Exposing the vulnerability of the car was. Exposing just how vulnerable the car was – THAT was what this person wanted to do."

Alisha scrambled to Nishant's office.

Nishant heard her out and gasped. There was someone on the team who was desperately trying to tell the car company that their cars had too much power under AI. That the very same AI could be hacked to kill people.

But the company pushed ahead with its AI development.

Who was that person?

They decided that Chris, Sarah, or Josh would not share any information voluntarily. So, people who had left the company in 2021 or thereabouts (shortly after the AI capabilities were enhanced) were called in. Did they remember an engineer or project manager warning about the need for safeguards in AI deployment? And being ignored?

Two names popped up – Chris and Sasha. Chris had remained with the company, while Sasha had resigned and now worked with children. They had married in 2019 and now lived close to the engineering office. Chris was still part of the AI development team. He had been a developer in 2018 and had slowly risen through the ranks.

Alisha let out a whistle, "Chris!"

In her head, the mental note read, "There is a reason that Philip is the top cyber cop in the world."

When questioned, Chris confessed readily enough.

"Yes, I wrote that script. I just never expected it to go on for so long. I thought that with the first car crash in China, they would be forced to sit up and do a code review. They did nothing.

Before injecting the script, for 6 months, I kept pleading with them to put a human override in the AI-led autopilot feature being developed. I begged them to have a basic security protocol in place for the AI engine that we were using in self-drive. Do you know what they did? They used that budget to start recording what people were saying in their cars! It was disgusting and voyeuristic.

I told them that with AI, we were building systems that were, in turn, hackable. But because these were smart engines, tracking a hack would be next to impossible. They wouldn't listen!

Honest to God, I never thought it would take them this long. I am sorry. For everything. But trust me, for the 100-odd people who have died because of me, thousands have been saved because you found that script and removed it. If this can put some kind of standards around how AI is secured in large implementations, I will be happy to spend the rest of my life in jail. Sasha and I have been expecting this. That's why we don't have kids."

The team was dumbstruck.

Nishant did not know whether he wanted to charge Chris or the CEO of the car company. The CEO was going to ignore the next security warning too. Chris, on the other hand, was just trying to scream his way to attention.

No one knew what to do. They called Philip. Philip heard them out, and then said, "Hold on to Chris, but treat him well. I have a few calls to make. I'll be in touch. Let everyone who is not needed for the next 24 hours go home and rest."

The team brought Chris dinner and some treats. They took care of him. Sasha came in to meet Chris. They gave them privacy.

In the meantime, keyboards were getting used at maniacal speed in many parts of the world. Phones were ringing. People were being pulled out of beds and brought to office. Ten hours later, it was a beautiful morning. The global CEO of the luxury car company had been "detained". The luxury car company had issued a notice to recall all cars fitted with this AI feature. They were never going to recover from that. Even as things stood, they were sure there wasn't enough money to pay customers compensation for the recalled cars, and a class action suit was likely in the US.

The Board of the company had resigned overnight. Yet, lawmakers were in consultation to figure out a way to hold them responsible for not demanding that the car company should internally investigate these crashes.

When the news of the recall broke, both AI and financial analysts went into overdrive. Suffice to say that TV stations in half the world got their fodder for 24 hours.

Everyone connected with the case had to face charges and was sentenced. The CEO was sentenced to an exemplary 124 years in prison, no parole.

October 2026: Two Years Later

The International Standards Organisation (ISO) launched the ISO 26001 – Ethical use of AI in IoT, vehicles, and other human systems. This was the result of two years of hard work.

All human use systems like vehicles, connected devices, home assistants, home security systems, and any other application of AI had to conform to the standards.

Since any crime or breach in an AI system had the potential to hurt the entire world, the UN passed a resolution to give the Interpol exclusive jurisdiction over AI and crime based on its application. This meant that the luxury car company could no longer convince a poor country to accept and buy its vehicles. No country could buy vehicles that did not meet AI security and ethics standards, and any violation would be handled directly by the Interpol. There would be no extradition formalities. Anyone found violating the International Standards for Ethical AI would be arrested from any part of the world, directly by the Interpol or its operatives. The local government would be powerless to stop this arrest.

Chris spent many years in jail, and everyone confirmed that he was the happiest person they met.

[1] Assembly Language is a kind of language that computers understand, but humans cannot. Computers only understand 0 and 1. So, all programs written by us are converted into machine language (the language that can be understood by a computer). Before text based computer programming languages were created, these programs were punched into punch cards and fed into the computers. Assembly language was also coded this way.

[2] When a person works alone, usually in a negative job, or in something like espionage, they are called a lone wolf.

[3] The release log maintains a list of the version and the date on which it was made live.

Epilogue

Hope you enjoyed the stories.
> Will you please take a minute to share your feedback?
> **hello@mytcp.in**
> If you are reading an ebook, just click here:
> https://quizizz.com/join?gc=49950903
> (takes less than a minute!)